# Prakash Kannan's
# Let's Walk

Prakash Kannan

## Also by Prakash Kannan

I Don't care

Why Me! When love meets reality

Prakash Kannan

# LET'S WALK



ISBN - 978-93-5469-042-6

*"Sometimes two souls meet not to stay together,
but to remind each other how it feels to be alive,
even if only for a while."*

*"Sometimes the Walk matters more than the
destination"*

*— Prakash Kannan, Let's Walk*

# AUTHOR'S NOTE

There are stories that we write and then there are stories that write us.

*Let's Walk* was one such story.

It began as a whisper in my mind an image of two strangers walking together on a rain-soaked evening, not saying much, but somehow understanding everything. They became Aditya and Mira. He, the stillness of thought. She, the rhythm of emotion.

Through them, I wanted to explore the beauty of unspoken love, the kind that doesn't always reach its destination but still defines the journey. Because not every connection is meant to end in forever; some are meant to remind us of who we were meant to be.

In my earlier books *Why Me! When Love Meets Reality*, and *Maybe That Was Enough* I've always tried to capture the quiet truth about relationships: that love is rarely perfect, but it's always profound. *Let's Walk* is perhaps the most personal of them all not because of the characters, but because of what they represent.

This book is about movement of time, of emotions, of life itself. It's about those who stayed, those who left, and those who still walk beside us in ways unseen.

And if, somewhere in these pages, you find a reflection of your own walk of someone you once met, loved, or lost then the story has already found its meaning.

Thank you for walking with Aditya and Mira.

And thank you for walking with me.

— **Prakash Kannan**

# ACKNOWLEDGMENT

No story truly belongs to one person. *Let's Walk* exists because of many hearts that crossed paths with mine.

To the quiet listeners, the late-night conversationalists, and the friends who walked with me through the cities that inspired this book - Bangalore, Delhi, and Mumbai, thank you for showing me that every street hides a story.

To those who believe in simple moments a shared coffee, a metro ride, a walk after rain, thank you for reminding me that love lives in ordinary things.

To my readers old and new who have stayed with me through *I Don't Care*, *Why Me! When Love Meets Reality*, and *Maybe That Was Enough* your messages, and your reflections keep me writing.

To the people who became pieces of my characters knowingly or unknowingly this is as much yours as it is mine.

And finally, to those we've lost to those who couldn't stay but still walk beside us in silence *Let's Walk* is for you.

— **Prakash Kannan**

Prakash Kannan

# Table of Contents


Metro ....... 1
Kurta ....... 9
The Notebook ....... 16
Mira ....... 28
New Routine ....... 34
Gulmohar Tree ....... 41
Shared Umbrella ....... 45
Filter Coffee ....... 58
To Do List ....... 68
The Good News ....... 75
Not the Good News ....... 82
The Ring ....... 88
A Trip ....... 94
The Unsaid ....... 98
Mutual Friend ....... 115
The Calling bell ....... 122
Fate of Unsaid ....... 129
Misconception ....... 135
Dinner ....... 144
Search ....... 157
Mumbai ....... 172
The Unsaid - Poems ....... 180
Full Circle ....... 190
Let's Walk ....... 195

The Real - Mira ........................................................................ 200

Epilogue ........................................................................ 216

# Bengaluru Part - 1

# Metro

The alarm went off at exactly 6:00 AM, just like every other weekday. I didn't need to set it anymore. My body knew the rhythm by now. Still, I let the buzzing continue for a few seconds, holding on to the last threads of sleep before reaching out from under the blanket and silencing it. The room was quiet, save for the distant sounds of the city gently waking up beyond the walls of my two-bedroom apartment near Ulsoor Lake, Mahatma Gandhi Road.

My mornings were predictable. Comforting. Simple. I moved like clockwork freshened up, brewed a quick cup of strong coffee, scrolled through unread news headlines, then stood by the small balcony to breathe in the early light. From up here, I could see the hazy outlines of the city's heart beating to life. The first few BMTC buses roared past, still mostly empty. The street vendors below were beginning to spread their tarpaulins and set up their carts. I spotted the flower seller who always arrived first, her hands a blur as she strung jasmine garlands while humming to herself. It was oddly soothing.

By 7:45 AM, I was dressed and ready. Simple shirt, dark jeans, canvas shoes. My backpack was light just my laptop, a water bottle, and a snack box. I locked up and made my way down the narrow staircase to the main road.

MG Road Metro Station was only a fifteen-minute walk. The air, still cool from the night, carried the faint scent of filter coffee brewing in nearby homes and the sweet fragrance of jasmine from the garlands sold at the small flower stall near the station entrance. The steps leading to the elevated station were already bustling. Students with heavy backpacks, officegoers clutching their lunch bags, and the occasional early bird vendor – a cross-section of the city converging on this lifeline. I swiped my smart card at the gate, a familiar access in my morning routine. The escalator hummed, carrying me up into the cool, echoing space of the platform.

By the time I reached the platform, it was 8:20 AM. The morning sun had begun its daily climb, turning the sky a muted shade of gold. MG Road Metro station during peak hours was a symphony of urban life. The rumble of approaching trains, the chatter of commuters in Kannada, Tamil, Hindi, Telugu, Malayalam and English, the announcements echoing through the speakers – a vibrant mix that usually faded into a dull background hum for me. The platform buzzed with quiet activity commuters standing in clusters, headphones plugged in, eyes either fixed on phones or lost in thought. I joined them. I always gravitated towards the less crowded end of the platform, near the signage for the MG Road line. My usual spot was near the end of the platform, close to the edge but not too close. I liked being able to see the city as the train glided forward. Around me, people were engrossed in their own morning routines scrolling through phones, sipping from thermos bottles, adjusting ties, whispering hurried last-minute reminders to children. The train's arrival was always the same: a deep rumble growing louder, then a soft whoosh as it pulled in, its metal body gleaming in the pale lights of the station. The doors opened with a hiss. I stepped in with the practiced ease of someone who had done this a thousand times. I found a place by the window and leaned against the glass. The seats were mostly taken, but the crowd wasn't unbearable yet. It was the silent hour, everyone awakes, but not quite ready to talk.

The train pulled out of MG Road and began its slow rise along the track. Outside the window, Bangalore transformed into a rapid blur of colors and shapes. Elevated metro bridges crisscrossed the skyline like giant skeletal structures. Inside, it was a crowded cocoon. Each person was wrapped in their own little world. Phones lit up faces in a soft blue glow. A man in a white shirt stood still, eyes closed, perhaps meditating. A teenage girl read a novel, mouthing the words as her finger moved along the page. Two college boys whispered over a shared pair of earbuds, occasionally grinning.

I put on my own headphones. A Hindi indie track filled my ears, a slow, melancholic tune that I had grown fond of. It was a simple song, but something in its lyrics made the world around me feel more distant, less intrusive. Music wasn't just sound. It was my armor. A way to keep the world at bay. The crowded metro didn't feel quite so overwhelming when I was tucked inside a melody of my choosing.

Trinity Station came and went in a blur. A few people got off. Some more got in. I had memorized the sequence, the exact timing between stops. It was a routine so ingrained that I could almost navigate it blindfolded. And with each stop, more faces, more stories, more silent narratives entered and exited my confined world.

At Halasuru, a young man carrying a guitar case got in and sat across from me. He looked sleepy but content. I envied that kind of ease. I used to have it once back in college, before the job offers and paychecks turned life into a series of checklists.

As we pulled into Indiranagar, the carriage began to fill. Students with overflowing backpacks. Officegoers with ID cards already swinging from their necks. One woman wore a deep maroon saree and stood holding the railing, eyes closed, lips moving in silent prayer. A man beside her scrolled through his phone, his brow furrowed with invisible worries.

I often found myself studying the reflections in the window, people's faces overlapping with the buildings flashing by. A woman applied eyeliner, her hand steady despite the gentle rocking of the train. A man held onto a pole with both hands, his wedding ring shining, his expression blank. A child giggled from the arms of his mother; the sound so joyful it cut through the usual silence.

Everyone was going somewhere. Everyone had a story, even if I didn't know what it was.

I never spoke. I never reached out. But in the silence, I found strange comfort like watching the ocean from the shore, feeling the weight of the waves but not needing to be in them. In some ways, the metro felt like a social contradiction. You were never more surrounded by people than in a packed train car, and yet, you could feel utterly invisible. That invisibility was both comforting and sad.

Sometimes I wished I could reach out to someone, say a simple "Good morning" or offer a smile that didn't feel awkward. But years of routine and invisible walls kept me folded into myself. I wasn't unhappy. But there was a quiet ache, like missing something you couldn't name.

My fingers adjusted the earphones. The music was slow, filled with soft piano and lyrics that sounded like letters never sent.

Then came Swami Vivekananda Road. The train slowed as it approached. The platform here always felt more crowded. It was strange how this chaos repeated daily, yet everyone accepted it. Like we had all signed an unspoken agreement to get through the commute quietly, to endure the discomfort, to coexist silently.

A mother boarded with her daughter maybe five years old. The little girl held a Barbie bag, pink and shiny. She was chattering nonstop, but her mother's face looked drained, her eyes sunken with exhaustion. Yet, every few minutes, the woman smiled and nodded, trying to match the child's energy.

That smile. I saw it on many faces in the metro. The tired-but-still-trying smile. The "I'm okay" smile. The "I have no choice but to keep going" smile.

I realized that I wore that smile sometimes too.

Behind every polite nod, every yawn, every bored expression in the carriage, there was a story of effort, of endurance. Some people looked forward to work. Others dreaded it. Some were heading to jobs they hated but needed. Some had lovers waiting. Others had nobody at all.

But here they were, all trapped inside the same metal box moving on steel tracks, pretending they weren't thinking anything too deep.

Sometimes, I imagined what would happen if people broke that code. What if someone started crying? Or singing? Or asked, *"How are you, really?"*

Would the carriage panic?

Would people look away?

Would someone answer?

I'd never dared to test it.

Finally, Baiyappanahalli. My stop. The Final stop as well.

I stepped out dodging elbows and heavy bags. The noise here was louder, less filtered. The station swarmed with bodies: students, techies, vendors, security guards, all merging into one river of movement.

Outside, I found an auto-rickshaw quickly. The driver nodded when I told him the name of the tech park. No questions, no conversation. Just the hum of the engine and the unpredictable dance of Bangalore traffic. We weaved through tiny lanes filled with honking, shouting, moving bodies.

My office tower rose like a giant from the earth, all glass and ambition. Inside, everything was sleek: polished floors, glass doors, card-access elevators. Yet the work itself was predictable: discussions, reports, meetings, emails, documentation. I was good at it, but not passionate. Work was what it always was: structured, efficient, quiet. The cold glow of monitors. Clicks and taps and muted pings. Emails that needed answers. Reports that needed fixing. People who smiled but kept their distance. I liked it that way. I liked the predictability, the order. Solitary affair in the office cafeteria, a functional refueling before diving back into the vast, impersonal digital world. Conversations with colleagues were polite, transactional, rarely venturing beyond work projects or the latest tech news. There was an unspoken agreement, a comfortable distance maintained between us, our interactions largely confined to the professional sphere.

But sometimes, especially after lunch when the world outside the glass windows shimmered, I felt a strange emptiness. Like I was moving but not arriving anywhere. Like I was doing everything right but feeling none of it.

Evening came slowly. I packed up at 5 PM sharp and retraced my steps. Auto. Baiyappanahalli. Metro. The return journey was slower, heavier.

The train was louder now filled with yawns, tired eyes, loosened ties, and bags slung lower on shoulders.

Even the music in my headphones felt softer, more introspective. I didn't lean on the window this time. I just sat and let the city flow past. The crowd pressed closer. The fatigue was shared. I recognized it in the way people slumped into seats or leaned against doors. The trip back home in the evening was a reverse replay of the morning, a mirror image of the crowded trains and familiar stations.

Back at MG Road, I stepped off and walked home. The breeze had picked up a little. The smell of roasted corn drifted from a street cart. I passed the same flower seller, now packing up her unsold garlands, humming the same tune from the morning.

I dropped my bag at home, changed into a t-shirt, and stepped back out. This was the part of the day I didn't skip. No matter how tired I was.

I stepped out for my walk at 6:30 pm.

My feet always led me down the same road, past the bookstores, past the park with the broken bench, into the quieter lanes of Ulsoor that the city hadn't swallowed yet. The noise faded as I walked deeper in. It was like slipping underwater.

There was an old house at the corner with a mango tree in the front yard. Its gate was always open. A boy once waved at me from the porch. I never saw him again. But I still looked every time I passed.

Children played cricket in narrow lanes, their laughter bouncing off walls. Elderly couples walking slowly, slowly discussing. Street dogs trotted behind garbage vans like curious citizens. The corner tea stall sizzled and hissed with hot oil and boiling milk. Steam curled into the air like incense.

These walks were my escape. My reset. They gave me space to think, to remember.

Sometimes, I thought about my father. A quiet man. Loved numbers. Rarely spoke unless it mattered. I remembered how he once told me,

"Loneliness isn't always a curse. Sometimes, it teaches you who you really are."

I hadn't understood it then. I think I do now.

There were moments - small ones - when a sound, or a smell, or a familiar sight would take me back. To days when I was a boy chasing kites on the terrace. To the first time I rode a cycle without falling. To the way my mother called my name when dinner was ready.

Life was quieter now. More still. I didn't mind the solitude. But sometimes, when I walked under the streetlights and saw other people talking, laughing, holding hands, I felt a twinge of something I couldn't name. Not envy. Not sadness. Just a soft ache. Like music heard through a closed window.

That night, I paused under the old banyan tree that stood near the end of my route. Its roots hung low like whispers. I looked up at the sky a faint silver moon barely visible through the clouds.

I stood there for a while, listening to the rustle of the leaves.

Something in me shifted that evening. It wasn't dramatic. It wasn't loud.

It was a small, quiet ripple.

Like the silence just before rain.

And as I turned onto that one quiet street the one, I always liked best, I felt something stir inside. A kind of quiet yearning. For what, I didn't know yet.

But it had begun.

And then, I walked home, unaware that tomorrow on this same street, under this same sky something would begin.

Something I hadn't planned for. Something small. Quiet.

But real.

# Kurta

I think it was a Tuesday. The air that evening in Bangalore was very cool. The day's heat was slowly giving way to the cooler evening, but the air still felt thin. My usual tiredness after work began to fade as I turned onto the quieter lane of the next street. The sky was painted with fading oranges and soft purples, a beautiful Bangalore sunset that often surprised me.

I was lost in my thoughts, going over a frustrating report I had gone through that morning. My footsteps made soft echoes on the mostly empty path. A single street dog walked past, its tail wagging slowly. The air carried the mixed smells of damp earth from a recently watered garden and car exhaust fumes.

I never used to notice people during my evening walks. Not really.

I noticed shadows, smells, colors, trees, the way streetlights flickered yes. But not people. Not faces. Not the way someone's presence could make the air feel… different.

Until her.

The first time I saw her, I hadn't expected anything unusual. It was just another Tuesday evening after another quiet day at work. The kind where every meeting felt like a repeat of the one before, and every column blurred into the next. My back ached from sitting too long, my brain dulls from too many tabs open.

I'd eaten dinner early that day: a simple bowl of oats and stepped out for my usual walk around 7:45 PM. I could see her that day because I changed by routine.

I turned onto the quiet lane that had become a part of my everyday rhythm. It was a street I liked. Narrow, slightly curved, lined with old houses and small gardens, with bougainvillea spilling over compound walls in wild shades of magenta and violet.

That's when I saw her.

A Glimpse in Red

She was walking toward me from the far end of the street, her figure slowly emerging from the shadows cast by tall trees and leaning fences.

And the first thing I noticed before her face, before her walk was her kurta. The fading light seemed to catch the deep red color of her kurta, making it almost glow in the twilight.

It was deep crimson.

The kind of color that doesn't shout but still holds your gaze. It seemed to glow slightly in the fading light, like a coal holding onto its warmth.

She wasn't in a hurry. Her steps were calm, steady. Her hair was dark and slightly wavy, rested over one shoulder and moved gently with each step. She carried a cloth bag, slung over her left shoulder, faded blue, with some small threads fraying at the edges.

There was nothing flashy about her. She wasn't trying to attract attention. In fact, she looked… at ease. Not distracted, not checking her phone, not talking to anyone. Just walking, like the road was hers and she knew exactly where she was going.

But somehow, everything about her made me pause.

As we came closer, I looked up, just briefly, not too directly. I didn't want to seem like I was staring. The gentle curve of her jawline, softened by the dimming light. She looked up too, but only slightly. Her gaze was lowered, thoughtful. Her expression unreadable, calm. The way she looked straight ahead, as if deep in thought. There was a tiny smile on her lips not one meant for anyone, just the kind that floats when your thoughts are elsewhere.

Her eyes, looking down as she walked, were framed by dark eyelashes.

Her eyes didn't meet mine.

But still, something flickered inside me. A small shift. A subtle pull.

And then, just like that, we passed each other.

No words. No gestures.

Only a moment.

We were on a path where we would meet, our ways coming together on this quiet road. My usual emotional distance changed slightly. It was surprising to see someone my age, walking at a similar slow pace, on this usually empty lane at this time

As we passed each other, it was a very quick moment, a quiet exchange between two strangers in the dying light of the day.

I caught a quick glimpse of her face, her smooth skin, the delicate arch of her eyebrow. Her expression was calm, almost thoughtful. And then, she passed me, her red kurta disappearing into the growing darkness.

The encounter was so brief and seemed so unimportant that it should have faded instantly, like a ripple in water. I kept walking, almost automatically, but my thoughts weren't with my feet anymore. They lingered behind on that red kurta, on the graceful way her arms swayed, on the unbothered confidence in her walk. A subtle change in the usual sameness of my evening walk. It was like a single, unexpected note in a familiar song, a slight difference that made me pause, even for a moment, in my usual thoughts.

I told myself it was nothing. Just one of those random, pleasant encounters that leave an impression for a minute, then fade. I'd probably forget about it by the time I got home.

But I didn't.

Her image stayed with me as I returned to my apartment.

It stayed with me as I switched off the kitchen light.

It stayed with me as I lay in bed, listening to the soft whirring of the ceiling fan.

And when I finally drifted off to sleep, somewhere between report and coffee and crimson cloth, I dreamt of a street that felt cooler than usual… and someone walking through it.

***

The next evening, the sky was a darker shade of purple as I started my walk, I told myself I was just going for my usual walk. A way to stretch my legs after hours spent sitting in front of a computer.

I followed the same route, the same streets, the same turns. My feet knew the way without thinking. But my mind?

My mind was more alert.

Every figure in the distance made my breath catch, just for a second. I caught myself scanning the path too early. Listening more carefully for footsteps approaching from behind. Looking a little longer than necessary when someone passed me.

I'm sure that it cannot be the same Crimson Kurta can be seen again.

And then like a trick of fate, like a small miracle she was there again.

A Cream-colored encounter. This time, she wore a cream-colored salwar kameez, with delicate embroidery near the hem. The fabric moved softly with each step. Her bag was the same. Her hair was loose, falling over her shoulders.

I noticed things I hadn't before.

She wore a tiny silver stud in her left nostril. Not flashy, just enough to catch the last rays of sunlight.

Her skin had a gentle warmth to it, like the tone of tea mixed with milk. Not pale, not dark just soft and earthy and glowing from within.

And this time, for a brief second, her eyes lifted.

They met mine.

It was fleeting, no longer than a breath, but it happened.

She didn't smile. Neither did I. But the acknowledgment was there.

Then she passed me again, walking into the same slow shadows as yesterday.

Questions With No Answers. I couldn't explain the way that second encounter made me feel. It wasn't excitement, exactly. It wasn't romantic, not yet. It was more like… curiosity. A gentle hum under the surface. A nudge. A whisper.

Who is she?

Where is she going?

Why does she walk alone like me?

It's strange, how quickly a stranger can find a place in your thoughts. You know nothing about them, nothing real but your mind begins to build gentle guesses. Imagined stories. Possible names. Occupations. Hobbies.

Maybe she was an artist. A teacher. A writer.

Maybe she liked quiet cafés and heavy books.

Maybe she had no idea I existed, and maybe that was okay.

But from that day forward, I hoped I'd see her again.

My Past Has Quiet Rooms.

That night, while brushing my teeth, I looked at myself in the mirror longer than usual.

Who was I to feel this sudden flicker of interest in someone? I'd spent most of my life avoiding entanglements. Preferring the safety of solitude. Comfort in routine. Emotions kept tucked away, like receipts in a drawer.

The last time I had been close to someone, really close was during college, Anu. She had been kind. Sharp-witted. Laughed easily. We had bonded over shared study nights and walks across the campus.

But slowly, life got in the way.

Different jobs. Different cities. A silence that stretched too long.

We never fought. We just faded.

And that hurt in its own way.

Since then, I'd built walls.

Not brick ones. Quiet ones.

Walls of timing. Politeness. Professional distance.

People assumed I was "reserved."

The truth was, I was just afraid of starting something I might not know how to hold on to.

A Strange Kind of Hope, But this.. this unexpected glimpse of a woman in a red kurta, had done something.

It had cracked a window open.

Let in a little breeze.

A little light.

It wasn't love. Not even close.

It was a shift.

Like someone had taken a familiar song and added a single new note.

And now, I couldn't stop listening for it.

Every day After, Over the next week, I walked at the same time, on the same road.

And more often than not, she appeared.

Sometimes in a blue kurta, sometimes white, once in a yellow dupatta that caught the wind like a flag.

Always alone.

Always calm.

We didn't speak. Not yet.

But the glances became more frequent. A tiny nod, maybe. A flicker of recognition.

And in that quiet dance of near anonymity, a new rhythm began to form in my life.

The walk was no longer just about movement.

It was about possibility.

# The Notebook

Somewhere along the way, the silence between us began to hold shape. It wasn't the kind of silence that weighed heavy, like an argument or an absence. It was a lighter thing. A silence that suggested something still forming, something just beneath the surface. Like a song whose melody you remembered, even if the lyrics escaped you.

The walks were the same. The route unchanged. The evening sky still painted with the hues of a city sighing into twilight. But now, I walked not only out of habit. I walked with intent.

And that intent had her face.

The girl in the crimson kurta, who now wore indigo or mustard or forest green, depending on the day. Her dupatta changing colors like seasons, her presence a steady note in the background of my life. A gentle rhythm. A pulse I couldn't unhear.

The ritual of my evening walk had slowly become the center of my day. What used to be a way to stretch my legs, to quiet my screen-tired eyes, had taken on a new shape. It was no longer just a walk. It was something else entirely.

It was about her.

Not that I ever admitted that to myself directly. Not out loud. But I felt it. The anticipation that hummed under my skin as the clock edged toward evening. The way my thoughts wandered toward her as I sat in yet another stand-up meeting or reviewed another page of financial report. I didn't know her name. I didn't know where she lived, or what she did, or why she walked at that exact hour on that exact lane. But I knew this: my days now had a before and after.

Before I saw her.

And after I started hoping I would again…

Every evening, I took the same route. Down the lane behind my building, past the house with the peeling yellow gate, past the sleepy dog who barely opened one eye as I passed. The same broken streetlight near the corner. The same slightly tilted red mailbox whose slot hadn't seen a letter in years. These were constants in my quiet world.

And then she became one too.

Not through grand gestures. Not through conversation. But through repetition. Through presence. Through silent recognition.

We had passed each other five times that week alone. She always walked with an effortless calm, her bag swinging gently at her side, her long hair moving softly with the wind. She looked like someone used to being in her own company. There was no phone in her hand, no earphones plugged in. Just her and the road.

I noticed the small things. How sometimes she paused briefly to look at a garden. How she occasionally glanced up at the sky. How once she stopped to tie her shoelace and didn't look around, fully unbothered by the world.

Once, she carried a book in her hand, not in her bag. It was a worn paperback with a cracked spine. I couldn't see the title. But it made me wonder what kind of stories did she like? Did she underline lines like I did? Did she fold corners, or did she use bookmarks? Was she the kind who wrote in the margins?

That week, though I saw her multiple times, our eyes met three times.

Three.

Brief. Measured. Not accidental.

And in those three glances, I felt something shift. Like a curtain being gently pulled aside.

We still hadn't spoken. Not a single word. But we had begun to exchange something glances, nods, slight smiles. Moments. Each evening brought the possibility of seeing her again. And each time I did, the world felt a little more textured, a little less grey.

She existed at the edge of things. Always walking just ahead, just beyond reach, yet always there. A part of the landscape of my days.

And maybe, just maybe, I had become part of hers.

***

It was a Tuesday when it happened. While evenings were soft and quiet, my mornings were mechanical. Wake. Shower. Coffee. Dress. Metro.

Morning, I walked to the MG Road station, my eyes half-open, music in my ears. The metro was my daily cocoon. I boarded the metro at MG Road around 8:35 AM, I was little late, missed 8:20 AM train. I'm with earbuds in, trying to zone out from the noisy shuffle of the world. I had grown used to standing by the window, letting the city blur past as I listened to the same playlist that marked the start of another day.

Most days, I avoided eye contact. People were tired. Phones were shields. Conversations were rare. I preferred it that way. Or I thought I did.

But one morning changed that.

As the train pulled out from Trinity, I noticed someone fumbling with a bag in front of me. A woman was adjusting the strap of her cloth tote as she stood up, preparing to get off at Halasuru. She turned slightly, and that's when it happened, a small notebook slipped from her bag and fell with a quiet thud to the floor.

I bent instinctively, picking it up. It was a modest thing, brown cover, stitched spine, slightly bent at the corners. There was no name on the front, only a tiny hand-drawn sun at the bottom right corner.

And then I looked up and it was HER.

She was the one the notebook had fallen from.

I froze.

Of course, I had imagined this moment a thousand ways. But never like this. Not here. Not with this sudden urgency in my hands, not with my mind racing to find the right words. My mouth opened.

"Excuse me" I said.

But the train had already come to a halt. The doors hissed open, and she stepped off her back turned to me completely unaware.

I moved forward, notebook in hand, but the crowd was thick, and by the time I made it to the door, it had closed again.

She was gone.

I stood holding the notebook, suddenly hyperaware of the weight in my hand, as if I were holding something more intimate than a belonging like a chapter of someone's life I wasn't meant to read.

The rest of my commute happened, technically. But my mind stayed right there on the platform, watching her vanish.

All I had now was a name-less, fragile brown notebook and the first real link between us

That evening, I didn't go for my walk. Instead, I sat at my desk, staring at the notebook. I didn't open it right away.

It felt too personal, like stepping into someone's living room while they were out buying milk.

But my fingers itched with curiosity. And somewhere inside, I knew this might be the only way I'd find her again. Or at least understand her better.

I finally opened it.

With hesitant fingers, I flipped it open.

The first page had her handwriting delicate, neat, and curved, like the wind had taught her to write.

A list of books.

A quote.

"Don't be afraid to start over again. This time, you're not starting from scratch, you're starting from experience."

Another page had a sketch of a tree, roots winding down into what looked like swirling words.

And then a poem:

> *"There are people you meet*
>
> *Who teach you silence*
>
> *Without asking for words*
>
> *Who look once*
>
> *And leave the world slightly tilted."*

It wasn't signed.

But it felt like her.

The rest of the pages were filled with similar fragments thoughts, reflections, lists of things she wanted to do. "Try filter coffee at that tiny shop near the temple," "learn to cycle again," "return library books (they won't arrest you)."

Then came sketches. A hand holding a cup of chai. A banyan tree with long roots. A pair of eyes half-lidded and thoughtful.

One page had a quote underlined:

"The quietest people have the loudest worlds."

I smiled. She was funny. Witty in a quiet way. Thoughtful.

Each page was a doorway into her mind. And I had walked right in.

Another had a poem.

> *I walk not to reach,*
>
> *But to stay in motion.*
>
> *To let the road rewrite*
>
> *What the day has tried to erase.*

She was a writer. Or at least a thinker. A chronic scribbler of thoughts.

I smiled.

This notebook was her inner monologue. I had stumbled into her private museum of ordinary wonders.

I couldn't read too much. I closed the book after a few pages, overcome by the intimacy of it all.

But something had changed in me.

I wanted to return it not just because it was hers. But because I wanted to be the one to give it back. To finally speak.

The next day, I got up earlier than usual. The metro was unusually packed. I boarded at MG Road again, the brown notebook carefully tucked in my bag, heart pacing faster than usual.

Notebook in my bag. Hope in my chest.

I stood at the same spot on the metro platform, heart pacing as if I was late for something.

But she didn't show up. I didn't see her on the platform.

Instead, someone else did.

As I adjusted my footing, a sudden voice cut through the usual silence of the coach.

"Welcome to another episode of 'Guess That Smell!' Is it body spray? Is it panic? Or is it yesterday's biryani in someone's lunchbox?"

Heads turned. People smirked.

I looked up.

He was tall, wearing a bright red shirt that clashed wonderfully with his turquoise sneakers, he looked like someone who had mistaken the metro for a stage, built like someone who might have once played cricket in college and never quite let go of that glory. Hair untamed, grin wide, eyes full of chaos.

He said to a woman who clearly had no interest in talking. "Just testing out my open-mic material. You know before I try it on my boss."

She turned away.

"Pranav," he whispered to himself, then grinned and turned to the guy next to her. "Tough crowd."

Then his eyes landed on me.

"Hi," he said to me directly, as if we were old friends. "You look like you've just written a breakup letter to your coffee machine."

I blinked.

"Too soon?" he asked. "You're a filter coffee guy, I can tell. Sensitive but loyal."

I shook my head, laughing quietly. "I prefer tea, actually."

"Ah, the poet's drink," he declared, clutching his heart. "You must be dangerous."

He thrust out a hand. "Pranav. Professional extrovert. Part-time designer. Full-time embarrassment to my family."

"You. You look like someone who silently judges people who put ketchup on dosa. Am I right?"

I stared.

He winked. "Don't worry. I'm with you. Ketchup has no place in South Indian cuisine. It's a hill I'll die on."

For the first time in weeks, I laughed like, properly laughed.

"I like you already," he said. "You've got 'quiet serial protagonist' vibes. Stoic. Brooding. Possibly poetic."

I blinked again. "What makes you think that?"

"You're carrying a brown notebook and haven't smiled until now. That's textbook."

I stared at the notebook in my bag.

He leaned back. "Relax. I'm not psychic. Just a people-watcher. Also, I talk too much. It balances out the universe."

And so, we talked.

Well, mostly he talked. But I found myself responding. Smiling. Laughing.

He asked about my work. My music. Why I always looked like I was contemplating the meaning of life while drinking black coffee.

By the time the metro reached Baiyappanahalli, I hadn't even realized we'd passed five stations.

"You've been upgraded," Pranav said. "From introvert in row three to human being. Proud of you."

And just like that, he vanished into the crowd.

That evening, I took the walk again.

And this time, I brought the notebook.

I didn't see her. Not on the road. Not by the curve near the tree. Not by the gate with the potted bougainvillea.

But I walked anyway.

I walked slower. With purpose.

I thought of her words. Her poems. Her unfinished lists. I imagined returning the notebook to her not in a rush, not as an accident, but in a conversation. With eye contact. And words.

I thought of Pranav too.

His unapologetic noise. His presence. How, in one metro ride, he had pulled me out of my own shell.

There were people who entered your life like sparks, lighting things up, even if just for a moment. And there were others who entered like shadows soft, subtle, yet impossible to ignore.

She was the latter.

He was the former.

And somewhere between them, I had begun to feel like a person again.

That night, as I turned off my light and pulled the blanket to my chin, I held the notebook one more time.

I hadn't written anything in it. It wasn't mine.

But it had become part of my story now.

And maybe soon, she would too.

Not as a silent figure on a quiet lane.

But as someone I could finally say hello to.

Maybe tomorrow, the silence would finally break.

Maybe tomorrow, the cadence would become a conversation.

It was a Thursday. I was running late, slightly annoyed that the water heater hadn't worked, and my shirt had a tiny stain I hadn't noticed until it was too late.

The metro was crowded. I stood by the door, adjusting my bag, preparing for another silent ride.

Then came him.

He entered like a gust of wind. Grinning. Tall. Loud. Confident. Not the irritating kind of loud, but the kind that immediately fills a room with warmth.

He looked around, scanning the faces. Then he caught my eye.

"You look like you've seen the code of the universe and are still unimpressed," he said, pointing at me. He thinks me as a software developer.

I blinked. Then laughed, a short, surprised sound that I hadn't expected from myself.

"Just a long week," I said.

"Aren't they all?" he replied.

He introduced himself as Pranav, a designer. Freelance. Occasionally employed, frequently caffeinated.

I said that I do remember him!

For the next few stops, he told stories about a client who wanted a logo that could be read upside down, about a cat that had followed him into the metro once, about his theory that the universe had a sense of humor but lacked subtlety.

People started to listen. Even the man beside me, who had been watching a video with headphones on, took one bud out to hear better.

Baiyappanahalli arrived too soon. "Well", Pranav said as I prepared to step out, "thanks for being my audience today. Don't let the code bite."

He gave a mock salute. And he asked by the way how people call you?

I said "My name is Aditya; few call me as Adi"

He said "Bye Adi"

And just like that, the doors closed, and he vanished. But something lingered.

A strange feeling.

That morning, I didn't feel like a ghost moving through routine. I felt like I'd been seen. Like the city, for once, had looked back.

That evening, my walk felt different. The sky was pale blue, slowly deepening as clouds gathered. The breeze was softer. The air smelled like earth and trees.

And then, from a distance, I saw her. She was wearing a navy-blue kurta this time. Her bag slung over the opposite shoulder. She looked thoughtful, maybe even tired. But still composed. Still present.

And when we passed, our eyes met again.

And for the first time, I smiled. Just a small smile.

The kind that says: I recognize you.

To my surprise, she smiled back.

Just a flicker. But it was real.

The first crack in the silence.

That night, as I lay in bed, I kept thinking about Pranav.

How easy it had been for him to connect. To break the invisible walls that so many of us carried. How the carriage had felt alive just because someone dared to speak.

And I thought of her.

How, without saying a word, she had changed something in me. Made me look forward to a moment that lasted less than a minute.

I realized that both things could be true: Words could light up a day.

And silence could hold the weight of a world.

Next evening, Friday. I walked again.

Notebook in hand. Breath measured.

And there she was coming around the same corner, same slow walk.

She looked a little tired. Her black dupatta barely clung to her shoulder. The notebook was absent from her bag.

I moved a little closer. This time, on the same side of the road.

She noticed me approaching just slightly.

And then our eyes met.

For a moment, I forgot how to breathe.

I stopped. She slowed.

And I held out the notebook.

She blinked. Her gaze fell to the cover. Recognition bloomed slowly, then her eyes widened just slightly.

"Oh," she said softly. Her voice. That was the first time I heard it. And it wasn't anything extraordinary. It didn't echo like music or sparkle like film. It was just… human. Cool breeze. A note that fit perfectly in the music I had imagined all this time.

"You dropped it," I said.

She took it, fingers brushing mine, and nodded. "Thank you."

Silence.

A beat passed. Then another.

"You read it?" she asked, not accusingly, just curious.

"A few pages," I admitted.

She gave a small smile not offended, not surprised. "Then I guess you already know too much."

I smiled back. "Just enough to want to know more."

For the first time, we both stopped walking.

And for the first time, it felt like we might walk in the same direction.

# Mira

"I guess you already know too much," she said with a smile, her fingers resting on the notebook's worn cover. "Just enough to want to return it," I replied.

For a moment, neither of us said anything more. The city continued around us traffic droned, footsteps echoed against walls, birds darted between bougainvillea vines, a dog barked in the distance but in that moment, the world had narrowed to a little stretch of pavement between us.

She hugged the notebook gently to her chest, and I could see the shift in her shoulders a slight relaxation, like someone settling into their own skin after holding their breath too long.

"I'm Aditya," I offered. My voice sounded quieter than I expected. Rough, maybe, from disuse.

She looked at me again. "I'm Mira."

Mira.

Of course it was. A soft name. It felt right in my mouth. Like something I'd known long before I heard it.

"I wasn't sure if I should open it," I said, eyes on the pavement. "But… it was the only way I'd know how to find you."

Mira smiled, a little shyly. "It's okay. If you hadn't, I'd have probably just thought I lost it forever. I don't usually drop things. That morning was chaotic."

We began walking, slowly, without talking about it. She matched my pace easily, or maybe I matched hers.

The silence between us wasn't awkward this time. It was just… careful. Like we were both feeling out the edges of a conversation neither of us wanted to break too quickly.

"What made it chaotic?" I asked after a few minutes, still watching the road.

She glanced sideways. "Just one of those days. Spilled coffee. Almost missed the train. Thought I lost my phone, but it was in my other bag. That kind of thing."

"Those days should be illegal," I said.

She laughed. A proper laugh. Not loud, but whole. Unpretentious.

"And you?" she asked. "You looked… completely calm. Like you were carrying that notebook on purpose."

I raised an eyebrow. "I was. I just didn't know how to give it back without sounding like a stalker."

She stopped walking briefly, then caught up with me.

"You didn't," she said. "You don't."

Her voice had something steady in it. Honest.

And just like that, the last of the tightness in my chest began to ease.

We turned onto the smaller road lined with houses old ones, single-story, with gardens that had grown wild over the years. Some had fences made of painted iron, others just low brick walls. There was a smell of something sweet in the air jasmine maybe, or someone cooking semiya in ghee.

"Is this your usual route?" I asked.

"It is now," she said, glancing at me with a sly smile. "You?"

"Yeah. Kind of my sanctuary after work. Helps me stay sane."

"I get that," she nodded. "I used to walk just to clear my head. Now I walk because… I like observing the way things change. Like this house," she pointed at a small yellow one with cracked tiles, "had its gate painted blue last month. And this tree" she touched a low branch as we passed "has started blooming late this year."

"You notice a lot."

"I have to," she said. "I forget everything otherwise."

I paused.

"Same," I said, almost without thinking. "Except I write it in balance sheets. Or bury it in playlists."

"Better than burying it in silence," she said, softer.

And I knew she didn't mean noise.

We stopped near the park at the edge of the road. The swings creaked with the slow, deliberate rhythm of dusk. A child's laughter rang out. Two uncles argued in low voices over a game of chess played on a stone table.

I turned to Mira.

"Do you always walk alone?" I asked.

She considered the question. "Not always by choice. But… yes."

I nodded. I knew that kind of alone.

"The notebook," I said, gently, "it said a lot. But it also felt like it left a lot unsaid."

Her eyes met mine. "Doesn't everything?"

She sat on a low bench and patted the space beside her. I joined her, cautiously.

"I didn't always write in it," she continued. "It started after I left my last job. I felt like I was… untethered. Like a balloon that had slipped from someone's hand."

"What did you do?"

"Communications," she said. "NGO. Storytelling, campaigns, community outreach."

I tilted my head. "That sounds like a lot."

"It was," she said. "Until it wasn't. I burnt out. I got tired of turning pain into narratives. So I quit."

"And now?"

"I joined another office, I freelance. And I walk. And I write. About anything. Or everything."

I didn't say anything for a while. We both watched a street dog digging near the roots of a Gul mohar tree, its paws kicking up orange petals.

"I met someone yesterday," I said, breaking the lull.

She looked at me, curious.

"On the metro. This guy named Pranav. Extremely extroverted. Loud. Funny. Ridiculously alive."

Mira laughed. "That sounds exhausting."

"It was. But in a good way. He joked about people's perfumes and scolded his imaginary boss out loud. Made everyone laugh."

She smiled again. "I envy that. That kind of ease."

"Same," I said. "He made the entire train feel less… robotic."

"Do you always talk to strangers?"

I shook my head. "Never. That was a first."

"What made you respond?"

I thought about it. "I think… he reminded me that we don't always have to be silent. That not all conversations need to be heavy or significant to matter."

She nodded slowly. "I think I've built so many walls around myself that I forget people can just knock."

"Well," I said, glancing at her, "I didn't knock. I returned lost property."

"That's the most introverted way to start a friendship," she grinned.

I grinned back.

We walked again.

The road was quieter now. Somewhere nearby, a pressure cooker hissed.

"Why did you keep walking past me all those days?" Mira asked, not confrontationally, but out of curiosity.

I shrugged. "I didn't know if I was allowed to say hi."

"You're allowed," she said.

"Even when you looked so composed. Like you were walking inside a poem?"

She laughed again. "That's just because I'm good at pretending I don't notice people."

I smiled. "Same."

We turned a corner. Her building was up ahead. A modest place with rusting balconies and a creeper vine climbing up the side.

"This is me," she said, slowing to a stop.

I stopped with her.

She looked at me. "Thank you. For the notebook. And for not being weird about it."

"I was a little weird about it," I admitted.

"Just the right amount," she said.

A pause.

"Will I see you tomorrow?" I asked.

"I walk every evening," she said.

I understood what that meant.

I nodded. "Then I'll Walk too."

***

That night, everything felt different.

My apartment, once echoing with loneliness, now felt like it held something different. My playlist felt new. My tea tasted softer. Even the traffic below seemed less like an assault and more like the breathing of a living city.

I sat by my window and opened my own notebook the one I hadn't touched in weeks.

And I wrote:

"Some silences are doorways.

Others are just waiting to be opened."

# New Routine

After I learned her name, the world shifted ever so slightly. It's strange, how something as simple as a name can change the texture of everything. For weeks, she had been only "her" in my head: the girl with the quiet walk, the girl with the notebook, the girl whose silence echoed like music. But now she was Mira.

That night, everything was different. The silence in my apartment wasn't empty anymore; it was full of Mira's laugh, the way she smiled, and the soft feeling of her presence. The words I had written in my notebook felt true. It wasn't a poem, just a simple thought, but it felt more important than any reports I had ever written.

Mira.
A name that tasted like water, like something clear and inevitable. The syllables replayed in my mind while I rode the metro the next morning, clinging to the stainless-steel pole as the train lurched out of MG Road. I whispered it once, testing how it felt aloud, almost embarrassed by the intimacy of saying it where no one knew what it meant.

Mira.

The city didn't care, of course. Trinity station rushed past, its platforms crowded with students and hurried officegoers. My routine hadn't changed. But I had.

The metro ride, once just a chore, now felt like a part of a larger story. I still put on my headphones, but the music was different. It didn't feel like a wall anymore; it felt like a friend walking beside me. The familiar faces of the other commuters seemed less like strangers and more like fellow travelers.

At Indiranagar, the train filled even more, and I found myself standing shoulder to shoulder with strangers. That's when I heard him.

"Ladies and gentlemen," a familiar voice boomed, "please welcome your favorite unpaid entertainer, forced once again into public performance because his landlord won't reduce the rent."

I looked up. Pranav, the man with the loud laugh, in another carriage. He was talking to someone, and a small group around him was smiling. Seeing him didn't make me feel left out; it made me feel like I was part of the city's shared, quiet rhythm.

Of course. His turquoise sneakers were impossible to miss. He stood at the center of the coach as if it were a stage, arms spread wide, grin flashing like he had been born to make people laugh at 8:40 AM on a Monday.

"Oh no," muttered someone beside me, but I smiled despite myself.

When his eyes landed on me, he lit up. "Ah! My silent philosopher. You survived last week's ride. I was worried you'd implode from the sheer volume of human interaction."

I smirked. "Barely."

Pranav winked. "We'll fix that."

He launched into another routine: mocking the corporate posters plastered above the doors ("Who honestly believes a gym membership can make you happy when happiness is clearly a plate of idli-vada?"), joking about how even the metro escalators felt overworked, mimicking a Kannada news anchor introducing the day's chaos with melodrama.

And once again, time slipped. Baiyappanahalli arrived before I'd counted the stations.

"See?" Pranav said as we spilled out of the doors. "That's two journeys you didn't count. You owe me a coffee."

I opened my mouth to protest, but he had already disappeared into the crowd, like a magician after a trick.

When I got to my desk at work, the lines of balance sheets on my screen looked less like a problem and more like a puzzle to be solved. But work remained what it always was — a series of screens, blinking notifications, and voices in conference calls that blurred into static. I prepared reports, nodded through presentations. None of it felt new.

My lunch was still eaten alone, but the quiet was okay. It was a time to think about the evening, about the walk, about what I might say to Mira. My mind, which used to be filled with work worries, was now full of new thoughts, new feelings. It was a quiet joy, a small, secret happiness that stayed with me all day.

And yet every now and then, between lines of balance sheets, her name surfaced. Mira. I found myself thinking of her handwriting, the lists in her notebook, the poem about walking. I imagined her at her desk, wherever that was, scribbling something in the margins of a page.

It was distracting. But it was also… a relief. A reminder that there was a world beyond Jira tickets and sprint deadlines.

When evening came, I left the office faster than usual. The auto ride felt like an impatient drumbeat. And when I finally stepped into the quiet lanes of my neighborhood, the air smelled sweeter: part incense from a nearby temple, part frying pakoras from a street vendor.

That evening, I didn't feel the nervous energy I had before. It was replaced by a calm feeling of anticipation. I knew she would be there. I didn't need to wonder anymore.

I found myself scanning the street ahead before I had even reached the corner. And then, there she was.

Mira.

Her hair tied loosely, a few strands falling across her face walking towards me. She was wearing a soft yellow kurta, a color that seemed to catch the last light of the day and hold it. She saw me and her smile was real, without hesitation. like seeing a friend, she was happy to meet. And just like that, the street felt smaller, as if the world had rearranged itself to make room for this meeting.

"Hi, Aditya," she said, her voice soft and warm.

"Hi, Mira," I replied, and the words felt easy on my tongue.

We fell into step together, side by side. We didn't talk much at first. The silence was comfortable, not empty. It was filled with the shared understanding of our routine, the little history we had already built without saying a word.

"My day was better than usual," I said after a while, my eyes on the trees as we passed.

"Mine too," she said, without asking why. "It's funny, isn't it? How a small change can make everything feel different."

"I think it's more than a small change," I said, and for the first time, I looked at her directly. Her eyes were warm, and she didn't look away.

"Maybe you're right," she said.

At first, the talk was light. As we walked, we began to talk more. We talked about small things. The color of the bougainvillea flowers that spilled over a wall. The weather, the traffic, the strangeness of Bangalore's sudden rainstorms that vanished as quickly as they came. She told me about a tea stall near her lane that made ginger tea so strong it could "either heal your throat or burn a hole through it." I told her about the filter coffee stand near my office that still used brass tumblers and treated every customer like family.

But slowly, the talk shifted.

She asked, "Do you like your work?"

I hesitated. "It's… fine."

"Just fine?"

"I guess I never thought too hard about whether I like it. It pays the bills. It keeps me busy. Sometimes it feels like I'm writing instructions for a machine to dream on my behalf."

She laughed softly. “That’s bleak.”

“Maybe,” I said. “What about you?”

She shrugged. “I write. But not always for myself. Sometimes for clients. Sometimes for no one. It’s easier to tell other people’s stories than my own.” She told me about her work as a creative writer, how she loved finding the perfect word to describe something, and how her work was both her passion and her quiet place.

I looked at her. “Maybe you’re afraid of being read.”

She stopped briefly, considering. “Maybe,” she said. “And maybe you’re afraid of speaking.”

I couldn’t deny it. I smiled instead.

We found ourselves slowing down, not wanting the walk to end.

"It's like we live in the same city, but in different worlds," she said, looking up at the sky where the first stars were starting to show.

"Not anymore," I said, and the words just came out.

She turned to me and smiled. The smile was a little shy, a little soft, but it was honest. "No," she said. "Not anymore."

As we walked, I told her about a person whom I met on the metro. I told her about his loud voice and his jokes and how he had made the whole carriage feel alive.

"He sounded like a splash of color," she said. "I wish I could be like that."

"I think you're a different kind of color," I said. "A calmer, more beautiful one."

She didn't reply right away. She just walked with her head down, a small smile on her face. I didn't feel awkward. It was just a quiet moment between us. The air felt full of unspoken things, but they were good things.

As we walked, her words lingered. Afraid of speaking.

It wasn't untrue.

I thought back to college days, to conversations I never had, to friendships that stayed shallow because I rarely let people in. I remembered evenings at home when my parents spoke across me rather than to me, my father always working late, my mother always tired. I remembered how silence had become my refuge.

But Mira was different. With her, silence wasn't a wall. It was a bridge.

We walked for longer than we had before. We passed her building and kept going. Neither of us said anything about it. We just walked. The streetlights came on, casting a soft, yellow glow on the pavement. I realized I was paying attention to every detail of the evening, not just her. I noticed the sound of an old song playing from a radio in a house we passed. I noticed the smell of freshly baked bread. My senses, which had been turned down low for so long, were now awake.

We reached the small park where the road forked. Children still played cricket in the fading light, their laughter ringing like bells. The air smelled of dust and wet grass.

"This is where I usually turn back," Mira said, pausing.

I nodded.

We stood there, neither moving. The pause stretched, comfortable and fragile at once.

When we finally turned back, it felt like the end of a long, good story. We reached her building, and she stopped. The darkness of the night had fully settled now.

"I had a really good walk," she said, her voice low.

"Me too," I said. "Thank you."

She just smiled. "I walk every evening," she said, the same words from before. But this time, they weren't a statement; they were a quiet promise.

"Then I'll be here too," I said.

As she walked up the path to her door, I watched her. For the first time, I didn't feel a pang of loneliness. I felt a sense of peace. I knew that even when she was gone, her presence would stay with me, a warm echo in the quiet of my apartment.

I walked home, and the street felt different. It was no longer a path for a solitary man. It was a path that led back to a promise, to a new beginning. My heart, which had been so careful and guarded for so long, felt lighter. I wasn't just walking anymore; I was walking with a purpose. And I knew that this walk was just the first of many.

That night, back in my apartment, I couldn't stop replaying the walk. Not the words, exactly, but the ease of them. The way conversation had come and gone like waves, the way silences didn't feel heavy.

For the first time in years, maybe ever, I felt the faint stirrings of something I hadn't dared to name.

Not love. Not yet. Something smaller, but more dangerous.

**Hope.**

# Gulmohar Tree

The street seemed to anticipate her before she arrived. Children were still playing cricket at the corner, their shouts sharp against the dusky air. A vendor pushed a cart of roasted peanuts, the smell of salt and smoke curling behind him. And then there she was.

Mira, she smiled when she saw me, and I felt something small but undeniable shift inside. We walked together as though we had always done so.

Her voice was lighter than the evening air. "You look less tired today."

"Blame Pranav," I said.

"The metro jester?" she asked, eyes glinting.

I laughed. "That's one way to put it."

She tilted her head. "You like him."

"Against my better judgment, yes."

She laughed, and the sound felt like the city itself exhaling.

We walked slowly, talking about nothing and everything. She told me about a book she had been reading, a collection of essays by a forgotten writer who observed small details about Bangalore in the 1970s. I told her about a film I'd seen long ago that had no dialogue at all, only the sounds of the city woven into music.

"You like silence too much," she teased.

"Maybe," I admitted. "But silence doesn't lie."

“Words don’t always lie either,” she countered.

She was right. But I didn’t say so.

There were moments, as we walked, when her questions nudged me toward places I rarely visited.

“Were you always in Bangalore?” she asked once.

“Yes,” I said, then paused. “Except for college, Chennai.”

“Did you like it there?”

I hesitated. “I don’t know if like is the word. It was… different. Bigger. Louder. I felt small most of the time. But maybe that was good.”

She studied me, as though listening to what I hadn’t said.

I remembered lonely hostel nights, the smell of wet clothes drying in corners, the laughter spilling from rooms I didn’t enter. I remembered professors who never knew my name. And I remembered one friend, a guy who had tried to pull me into his circle, who had laughed too easily, too brightly, almost like Pranav. I had let that friendship slip away.

“Small doesn’t always mean invisible,” Mira said quietly, breaking into my thoughts.

I glanced at her, surprised. But she only smiled.

We reached the park again. Children were now chasing each other in the fading light, their laughter rising and falling like waves. A few elders sat on benches, murmuring about politics, while a couple of dogs fought lazily over a discarded packet of chips.

We sat on the low stone bench near the Gul mohar tree.

“Do you ever write for yourself?” I asked, nodding at her notebook.

“Sometimes,” she said. “But mostly, I write to understand. It’s like… taking a mirror and tilting it until the reflection makes sense.”

I thought about my own work, about reports that never revealed themselves until you twisted them into the right shape. “I get that,” I said.

"Do you ever write outside of reports?" she asked.

"Not really. I used to, in school. Poems. But…" I shrugged. "It felt pointless after a while."

"Maybe you stopped too soon," she said.

Her eyes were calm but insistent, like she wasn't really asking but challenging.

***

Days began to fold into one another. Work in the morning, the metro with its chaos, sometimes Pranav's laughter, sometimes the blank stare of strangers. Evenings with Mira.

We began to map out pieces of each other. She told me about her childhood in Mumbai, about cycling down tree-lined streets and sneaking mangoes from her neighbor's garden. I told her about my father's obsession with punctuality, my mother's quiet strength, the Sundays when the three of us would share a meal that felt like a fragile truce.

Some evenings we spoke a lot. Other evenings we walked in silence. But the silence was no longer a gulf. It was a presence, something that belonged to both of us.

One evening, as we neared her building, she said suddenly, "You laugh differently now."

I blinked. "What do you mean?"

"It used to sound… reserved. Like you were afraid of how much space it would take. Now it sounds real."

I didn't know how to reply. I only smiled, and in that smile was an admission.

By the end of that week, I realized something unsettling.

I was waiting for these walks. Not casually, not as a pleasant routine, but as though they were the axis around which my day turned. Everything else: work, commute, even the rare bursts of laughter from Pranav, were just filler.

The walks were real. She was real.

And though we hadn't said it, though we hadn't even named it, I could feel it. We were at the edge of something.

Something that terrified me. Something that thrilled me.

# Shared Umbrella

The next evening, I left the office with that now-familiar sense of anticipation. The numbers and charts of my finance world: market fluctuations, quarterly reports, interest rates blurred into insignificance as soon as I stepped out of the building. Outside, the Bangalore sky was restless. Clouds gathered in uneven patches, heavy and bruised with the promise of rain. The air felt different dense, like the city was holding its breath.

By the time I reached our lane, the bougainvillea leaves were trembling in the wind. A boy hurried past on a cycle, balancing an umbrella that flipped backward in the gust. I smiled despite myself.

And then, there she was.

Mira.

She stood at the corner, notebook tucked under her arm as always, hair loose today, strands escaping across her forehead. She looked up and smiled when our eyes met. It was a small smile, but it struck me like sunlight breaking through a cloud.

"You came," she said.

"I always do," I replied, and it was true.

We began walking as we always did, step for step, unhurried. But the air had shifted; a crack of thunder rolled in the distance, echoing between the buildings. Mira glanced upward; eyebrows raised.

"Think it'll rain?" she asked.

"This is Bangalore," I said, smirking. "It's not a question of *if* only *when*."

We both laughed softly, but our laughter was quickly swallowed by the first few drops. Fat, heavy raindrops splashed onto the pavement, darkening the dust into patches of ink. Mira instinctively lifted her hand, palm open, feeling the rain like a child might.

"I love this smell," she murmured.

I inhaled deeply. The petrichor rose rich and earthy, mixed with the sharper scent of diesel from an auto passing by the faint sweetness of wet flowers from someone's garden.

And then the rain thickened. What began as scattered drops turned into a sudden sheet, falling hard, bouncing off rooftops, streaming down leaves, drenching the street in minutes.

We both broke into a run not far, just to the low awning of a closed bakery. The shutters were down, but the narrow strip of roof above jutted out enough to shelter us. We pressed ourselves close to the wall, shoulder to shoulder, watching the rain roar down in silver streaks.

The street had emptied quickly. Children had fled indoors, shopkeepers had dragged tarps over their wares, and traffic slowed to a crawl. For a few minutes, it felt like the city belonged only to us. Just me, her, and the relentless drumming of rain on tin.

Drops slipped from her hair onto her cheeks. She brushed them away, smiling. "Well… so much for an evening walk."

"I think we're still walking," I said. "Just standing still."

She gave me a look: half amused, half thoughtful. "That's such an Aditya thing to say."

"And what does that mean?"

"It means you notice things… but you'd never admit you want to."

I let the words hang in the air. She wasn't wrong.

The silence that followed wasn't awkward. It was heavy, yes, but not suffocating. There was something about the rain the way it cloaked the world, made every sound distant that made our closeness feel more intimate.

After a long pause, she spoke, her voice quieter than before.

"I have an interview tomorrow."

I turned to her. "Interview?"

She nodded, hugging her notebook closer. "Face to face. Not online this time."

"That's good," I said. "Means they're serious."

"Maybe." Her eyes flickered to the rain. "It's been a while since I've done one in person. I'm nervous."

"You'll be fine," I said immediately. It wasn't a line of comfort it was certainty. Mira carried a quiet strength that I had no doubt would show itself when needed.

She smiled faintly. "You sound so sure."

"I am."

For a moment, I almost asked: *Where? Which company? What role?* But something stopped me. Maybe it was her tone: deliberately vague, as though she wasn't ready to give details. Maybe it was the look in her eyes, which carried both excitement and fear.

So, I didn't ask. I simply nodded.

"You'll do well," I said again, softer this time.

She looked at me, gratitude flickering across her face. Then she leaned back against the wall, watching the rain blur the street into watercolor strokes.

We stood there until the downpour began to soften, the sheets thinning into drizzle. The world slowly returned: children reemerged with plastic cricket bats, autos honked impatiently, a woman hurried by with her sari gathered above her ankles.

Mira adjusted her scarf, readying herself. “Looks like we can walk again.”

“Yeah,” I said, reluctant to leave the shelter that had felt like a pocket universe for just the two of us.

We stepped back onto the glistening road. Puddles reflected the neon glow of signboards. The air was cooler now, washed clean.

When we reached the fork near her lane, she paused. “Wish me luck for tomorrow.”

“You don’t need it,” I said. “But… good luck anyway.”

She laughed, waved, and disappeared down the lane.

That night, I couldn’t focus on anything neither the financial reports on my desk nor the half-hearted dinner I’d cobbled together. My mind kept circling back to her words.

*I have an interview tomorrow.*

Where? For what? Why hadn’t I asked?

But I didn’t regret holding back. Mira had offered me what she wanted to share. That was enough. For now.

Still, as I lay in bed, listening to the faint hum of traffic outside, I found myself hoping. Hoping it would go well. Hoping it would bring her closer to what she wanted.

I didn’t know then how close it would bring her to me.

***

The next morning at the office began like any other. Numbers glowed on screens, markets fluctuated in restless patterns, analysts debated in muted tones. I buried myself in spreadsheets, the safe monotony of finance.

Around mid-morning, I stepped out into the lobby for a coffee. And froze.

There she was.

Mira.

She stood near the reception desk, her notebook in hand, dressed in a crisp white kurta and a muted scarf. Her hair was tied neatly this time, professional, but her eyes carried the same mix of calm and nervous energy I'd seen the night before.

For a second, the world tilted. The sterile walls of my office, the gleam of marble floors, the muted hum of finance chatter none of it belonged to her. And yet here she was, impossibly, undeniably here.

She hadn't told me the company name. And I hadn't asked. But fate or whatever force guided these coincidences had brought her into my world anyway.

Our worlds. Colliding. She hadn't seen me yet. Mira stood near the glass-paneled reception, scanning her notebook, as though rereading her own scribbles for courage. A receptionist tapped at a keyboard nearby, indifferent. Two other candidates waited in the lounge; their resumes clutched in plastic folders. But my eyes only found her.

Mira, in *my* office.

The thought rattled me. Until now, she had belonged to evenings and bougainvillea lanes, to walks under Gul mohar trees, to rain-drenched shelters where silence felt shared. She was not supposed to exist among glass elevators, financial tickers running across LED boards, the low hum of analysts discussing derivatives.

And yet she did.

For a brief moment, I considered turning back, pretending I hadn't seen her. But something stronger pulled me forward.

"Mira," I said softly.

She looked up and her eyes widened. Surprise flickered across her face, followed quickly by something warmer, almost relieved.

"Aditya?" Her voice was quiet, but in the sterile office air, it felt like a chord struck too loud.

We stood facing each other, both caught between familiarity and strangeness.

"You… work here?" she asked, almost incredulous.

"Yes," I said, managing a smile. "Finance division. Numbers and spreadsheets. My… natural habitat."

She laughed softly, though it sounded nervous. "And here I was, trying to keep the company name a secret yesterday."

"Well," I said, "the city has a sense of humor."

For a moment, neither of us knew how to bridge the gap between who we were outside and who we were here. At work, I was expected to be composed, analytical, precise. Around her, I had been hesitant, thoughtful, even vulnerable. Which self was I supposed to be now?

"You didn't tell me," I said gently.

"I didn't think it mattered," she replied. "And maybe… I didn't want to jinx it." She looked around the lobby, lowering her voice. "I wasn't sure I could handle you knowing."

I understood. There are parts of us we don't want witnessed until we're ready.

"You'll be fine," I said, echoing my words from the night before. "You always are."

Something flickered in her eyes at that gratitude, or maybe faith.

She was called to sit with the other candidates in the waiting lounge. I hovered awkwardly, torn between retreating into my work and staying near her. From my vantage, I could see her flipping her notebook open, skimming pages where she had written reminders: *breathe, listen carefully, don't rush answers.*

My heart clenched. Mira, who spoke so easily of words and mirrors, who challenged me to speak more, was now preparing herself to be judged by my management.

I wanted to tell her she didn't need to prove anything. But in this world my office, my domain that wasn't true. Here, everyone had to prove themselves.

I sat down across from her, keeping my voice low.

"You're early," I said.

"I was too nervous to wait at home," she admitted. "So, I came sooner. Better to let the nerves out here."

I smiled. "That's smart. Less time for overthinking."

She raised an eyebrow. "You would know."

I laughed. "Fair."

The laughter softened the strangeness between us. For a moment, we were back under the bakery roof, listening to the rain. Except now the roof was glass, the rain replaced by fluorescent lights and the faint hum of the office AC.

As we spoke, colleagues passed by. Some glanced curiously at me—Aditya, usually reserved, sitting across from a woman in the lobby, smiling more than usual. I felt their eyes but ignored them.

Still, something gnawed at me. I realized that here, within the walls of my office, our bond looked different. Out on the lanes, we were equals two solitary walkers sharing silence. But here, she was a candidate, and I was already inside.

The thought unsettled me. I didn't want to be someone she looked up to, or someone whose approval mattered more than it should.

So, I pushed the thought aside.

Finally, her name was called. Mira stood, adjusting her scarf. For the first time since I'd known her, she looked unsure. Vulnerable, almost small.

"You'll do well," I said again, firmly, before she could step away.

She glanced back, and this time her smile was stronger. "Hold that thought."

And then she was gone, disappearing into the glass-walled corridor that led to the interview rooms.

I sat there longer than I intended, staring at the closed door, realizing my chest felt tight.

It was one thing to walk beside her under rain. It was another to see her enter my world, where numbers ruled, and human warmth often dissolved into quarterly targets.

And for the first time, I wondered: What if she became part of this world too?

When she disappeared down that glass corridor, the lobby felt hollow. I tried to return to my desk, but the rows of numbers on my screen seemed drained of meaning. Market graphs rose and fell with their usual rhythm, but my eyes kept flicking toward the clock. Each minute ticked slower than the last.

Somewhere beyond those doors, Mira was speaking. Answering questions, offering parts of herself to people who would measure and judge. And I, accustomed to measuring risk and profit, realized I hated that she had to be measured at all.

I pictured her sitting upright, hands steady on her lap, notebook tucked away, eyes meeting the panel with calm determination. But then I pictured the nerves, the tiny tremor in her voice, the way she sometimes bit her lip when uncertain.

I almost wished I could storm in there, tell them: *She's enough. Don't ask her to prove it. Don't try to quantify her worth like you do a balance sheet.*

But of course, I couldn't. This was the world I worked in, and in this world, numbers ruled.

I sat back at my desk, staring at spreadsheets but thinking of her words from our walks.

She once said writing was about tilting a mirror until the reflection made sense. Finance, I realized, was the opposite: taking chaos and pressing it into boxes, formulas, models that stripped away the messiness until only order remained.

Her world embraced uncertainty. Mine tried to erase it.

And yet here she was, crossing into my territory. What did that mean? Did she want to leave behind the world of words for one of numbers? Or was this just a steppingstone, a compromise, the way many dreams were reshaped into survival?

The thought unsettled me more than I wanted to admit.

When Mira finally reappeared, I stood instinctively.

She walked back into the lobby with measured steps, but her face betrayed a mix of relief and exhaustion. She saw me immediately, and her lips curved into a tired smile.

"It's done," she said softly.

I nodded. "How did it go?"

She exhaled, leaning slightly against the wall. "I think… okay. They asked a lot about adaptability, writing samples, the usual. One of them wanted to know how I'd explain complex financial terms to someone outside the field." She chuckled. "I told them I'd compare inflation to the way a plate of pani puri keeps getting more expensive each year."

I laughed. "That's brilliant."

"They laughed too," she said, eyes twinkling. "So maybe that's a good sign."

Her laughter echoed in the sterile lobby, softening its edges, making it feel less like a financial fortress and more like a space that could, just maybe, hold something human.

As we spoke, I became acutely aware of how strange this felt. Mira wasn't supposed to be here. She belonged to the evenings, to rain-drenched shelters, to Gul mohar lined lanes. Yet seeing her in this space made my office world feel different less rigid, less lifeless.

And with that realization came another: I didn't want her to vanish back into the rain-washed streets only to remain a visitor in my life.

Her presence here changed things. And maybe, I wanted them to change.

She gathered her things, thanked the receptionist, and turned to me. "Back to your spreadsheets?"

I smiled. "Unfortunately, yes."

"And I go back to waiting," she said, her tone somewhere between hope and resignation.

"Waiting?"

"For their reply." She paused, then added quietly, "For everything, maybe."

We walked toward the elevators together. For once, I didn't care if my colleagues saw.

Inside the lift, silence stretched between us, but it wasn't heavy. It was threaded with something new, a recognition that our worlds had overlapped, however briefly, and nothing would be quite the same after.

When the doors opened, she stepped out first.

"Good luck," I said again.

She glanced back. "You already gave me luck. Now give me coffee sometime instead."

The doors closed before I could answer, leaving me staring at my reflection in the mirrored walls, heart pounding in a way that numbers could never explain.

The office never felt the same after that morning.

Numbers blinked on my screen, market indices rose and fell, colleagues debated projections around me, but everything seemed dulled, muted, as if the entire building had been drained of color except for the brief space where Mira had stood.

I caught myself glancing at the reception more than once, half expecting to see her still there, flipping her notebook nervously, smiling faintly when our eyes met. But of course, she was gone.

Gone back into the city, into her words and her silence, while I remained trapped in the cadence of finance. And yet, something lingered. Her presence had left a mark on these sterile walls, like rainwater staining concrete, refusing to disappear.

Through the rest of the afternoon, I wrestled with an unfamiliar sensation. It wasn't just surprise at seeing her here it was disorientation.

Until now, I had lived with a clear partition: my work belonged to one world, rigid and measured; my evenings with Mira belonged to another, fluid and unpredictable. Two spheres of existence that never touched.

But now they had collided. And I didn't know what that meant.

Could I keep her in the quiet lane walks, safe from the glare of conference rooms? Or would she step into this space, reshape it with her words, her laughter, her mirror-tilting metaphors?

The thought filled me with both unease and a strange kind of hope.

By the time evening descended, the city was washed in the pale glow of streetlights. Clouds lingered still, heavy with leftover rain, and puddles mirrored the yellow orbs of lamps.

I walked quickly toward our usual lane, pulse quicker than usual. For the first time, I didn't know if she would come. Maybe she was too tired after the interview. Maybe she wanted distance from seeing me in that professional shell.

But then there she was.

Standing under the Gul mohar tree, looking as though she had always belonged there.

"You came," I said, relief leaking into my voice.

Her eyes softened. "Of course. You thought I wouldn't?"

"I wasn't sure," I admitted.

She tilted her head. "Because of this morning?"

I nodded.

"It was strange," she agreed. "Seeing you there. You were… different."

"How so?"

"More certain. More contained. Like you belonged to that place." She paused, then added, "And yet, you didn't."

Her words hit me harder than I expected.

We began walking slowly, our steps splashing through puddles. Children's laughter echoed from a nearby alley where they batted a soaked tennis ball back and forth. The smell of damp earth clung to the air, mingling with the faint spice of frying pakoras from a roadside cart.

"So," I asked carefully, "how do you feel about the interview now?"

She sighed. "Relieved it's over. But also… uncertain. They seemed interested, but who knows? I've learned not to pin too much hope on these things."

"You did well," I said firmly.

"You weren't in the room," she countered.

"I didn't need to be."

She smiled faintly at that, though her eyes flickered with doubt.

As we walked, the conversation shifted.

"You know," she said, "I always imagined finance as… distant. Cold. But sitting there today, watching people walk past in suits, staring at numbers there was something human in it too. Like behind every graph was a story someone forgot to tell."

I looked at her, startled.

"No one here would say that" I murmured.

"Maybe that's the problem," she said.

Her words lingered in the damp air between us.

By the time we reached the small park, the drizzle had returned; light, misty, more like a caress than rain. We sat on the familiar stone bench beneath the Gul mohar, red blossoms scattered like confetti at our feet.

Mira tilted her face upward, letting the drizzle touch her cheeks. "Funny, isn't it? Yesterday we hid from the rain. Today, I don't mind it."

"Because the interview's over?" I asked.

"Maybe. Or maybe because the rain isn't the same twice."

I watched her for a long moment, her words weaving themselves into me. The rain wasn't the same twice. Neither were we.

And in that moment, I knew Mira was no longer just a presence in my evenings. She was shaping the very architecture of my days, bleeding into spaces I had kept separate, loosening walls I didn't realize I had built.

When it grew darker, we parted at the fork, as we always did. She turned down her lane, waving lightly, notebook pressed to her chest.

I stood watching until she disappeared, the drizzle softening the outlines of the street.

Walking back alone, I realized something unsettling and exhilarating all at once:

It wasn't just about seeing her. It wasn't even about walking with her. It was about the way the world felt when she was in it.

And that world, I thought, was one I didn't want to leave.

# Filter Coffee

The next evening, I returned home carrying the fatigue of the day, the kind of weariness that clings more to the mind than the body. Numbers had blurred together: ratios, projections, endless discussions about risk mitigation. Finance drained you in ways you couldn't see; it was like being slowly hollowed out, one calculation at a time.

I had just set my bag down, unbuttoned the top of my shirt, when the doorbell rang.

For a moment, I froze. Nobody rang my doorbell at this hour. My life had been built around routine solitude colleagues during the day, silence in the evening. Visitors were rare, almost nonexistent.

I walked to the door, half-expecting perhaps a neighbor, or a delivery boy who had got the wrong address. But when I opened it.

"Mira?"

She stood there, hair loose, eyes bright with the afterglow of the evening. She held her notebook casually in one hand, but her smile was the thing that hit me first: wide, genuine, almost mischievous.

"Surprise," she said.

For a moment, I simply stared. The image felt too strange, too intimate: Mira, not on the street or in the park, but at the threshold of my home. The world we'd built so far had always belonged outside, to open skies and shared pavements. But now she was here, at my door.

I stepped aside. "Come in."

She walked in slowly, as though stepping into a secret. And then she stopped short, looking around.

"This is your flat?"

"Yes," I said, suddenly self-conscious.

Her eyebrows arched. "It's… clean."

I laughed. "What did you expect? Chaos?"

She grinned. "Honestly? A mess. A bachelor's lair. Clothes on the chair, dishes in the sink, empty pizza boxes, dust in corners."

"Well, sorry to disappoint you," I said dryly.

But she wasn't disappointed. She walked slowly through the small living room, her eyes scanning everything with the curiosity of someone entering a new chapter of a familiar book.

The bookshelves against the wall, arranged in neat rows. The potted plants by the window, their leaves catching the last light of day. The soft rug under the coffee table, the framed photograph of Cubbon Park I had once bought from an artist.

She turned to me, still smiling. "This doesn't look like a bachelor's place at all. It looks like…" She paused, searching for the word. "…like someone cares about living here."

I shrugged, uncomfortable under her gaze. "Plants don't water themselves."

"Maybe," she said, stepping closer to a small jade plant on the shelf, touching its leaf gently. "But not everyone remembers to water them."

***

We sat down she on the couch, me across from her. The air carried the quiet weight of beginnings, of newness. For the first time, we were in a space that belonged entirely to me, not to the city.

She looked around once more, then leaned back, her notebook on teapoy. “I didn’t know if I should come,” she admitted. “But today… I just wanted to.”

“I’m glad you did,” I said, surprised by how easily the truth came out.

Silence lingered a moment. Then she asked, “Do you ever think about marriage?”

The question startled me not because it came out of nowhere, but because it was so direct.

“Marriage?” I repeated, buying time.

She nodded. “Everyone keeps asking me about it lately. Friends, family. It’s exhausting.”

I leaned back, exhaling. “Honestly? I don’t think it’s necessary.”

Her eyes flickered with interest. “Why not?”

“Because it feels… performative. A contract society built to make people feel safe, to give them a framework. But love doesn’t need paperwork. Companionship doesn’t need rituals. If two people care for each other, that should be enough.”

She studied me. “You sound very certain.”

“I’ve seen marriages that were empty,” I said quietly. “People staying together because of expectation, not connection. I’d rather be alone than live like that.”

She didn’t reply immediately. She looked down at her notebook, tracing its edges with her thumb.

Finally, she said softly, “I don’t know what I think. I only know I don’t believe in arranged marriages. The idea of being matched, judged by checklists, introduced like products on a shelf, it feels wrong.”

Her voice was firmer now. “Love should happen on its own. Organically. Without forcing it. Otherwise, what’s the point?”

I nodded, watching her. She wasn't just answering me, she was answering invisible voices around her: her family, society, perhaps her own doubts.

"And marriage?" I asked.

She shrugged. "I don't know. Maybe someday. Maybe never. Right now… I'm not in a place to even think about it. I just want to live my life, write, figure things out."

Her honesty hung between us, fragile and raw.

She broke the silence first, with a sudden grin. "But right now, I'm just hungry."

I laughed, relieved. "That's easier to solve."

I led her into the kitchen, a compact space lined with jars of spices, a small fridge humming in the corner, and two more plants perched on the windowsill. She blinked at it.

"You actually cook?"

"I try," I said.

"Impressive," she teased. "I was expecting instant noodles."

"I save those for desperate nights."

We set about preparing a simple meal - vegetable upma, with roasted cashews for crunch. I chopped onions while she stirred, the rhythm of the pan filling the silence between us. Occasionally, our hands brushed when passing utensils, each touch light but charged.

It felt oddly domestic, intimate in a way the outside world could never be. Two people moving in a small kitchen, learning each other's pace.

At one point, she laughed as I fumbled with too much salt. "Finance guy, can't measure salt properly?"

"Numbers don't taste," I shot back.

We both laughed until our eyes watered.

We sat at the dining table, steam rising from our plates. Mira took her first bite, then looked at me with exaggerated seriousness.

“Not bad,” she said. “For a bachelor who allegedly cooks.”

I bowed slightly. “High praise.”

As we ate, conversation flowed more easily. She told me about an essay she had been working on about the sounds of the city, how each neighborhood carried its own rhythm. I told her about a colleague obsessed with predicting the next market crash, as though the future could be tamed with enough graphs.

It struck me that this sharing food, trading stories, felt more real than any definition of marriage I had ever considered.

After dinner, I hesitated before saying, “There’s something I want to show you.”

Curiosity sparked in her eyes. “What?”

“Come,” I said, grabbing my keys.

We stepped out into the cooler night. The drizzle had stopped, leaving the streets damp and reflective. I led her down the quieter lanes, past closed shops and the occasional chai stand still glowing.

Finally, we stopped outside a small filter coffee shop near the temple, one of those old, brass-tumbler places tucked between modern cafes.

She blinked. “Why here?”

“Because,” I said with a smile, “I remember something from your notebook.”

Her eyes widened.

“You had ‘drink proper filter coffee near the temple’ on your to-do list. Tonight, you can tick it off.”

For a moment, she just stared at me, as though I had reached into her private world and pulled out a secret, she hadn’t expected me to hold onto.

Then she smiled, slow and genuine, and it lit her face in a way that the shop's yellow bulbs could never manage.

"You remembered."

"Of course," I said.

We ordered two tumblers. The aroma was strong, earthy, cutting through the night air. As she took her first sip, she sighed in delight.

"Worth it," she said. "Completely worth it."

I laughed. "Now you can tick the box."

She pulled out her notebook, flipped to the page, and with a dramatic flourish, placed a checkmark next to the line. Then she looked up, still smiling.

"There are more things on the list," she said softly.

I raised an eyebrow. "More coffee?"

"Not just coffee," she replied. "Life."

And for the first time, I realized: her list wasn't just about tasks. It was about becoming.

***

We sat on the wooden bench outside the small shop, tumblers of steaming filter coffee warming our hands. The street was alive in its own quiet way autos slowing down, the hiss of frying from a nearby eatery, the occasional burst of laughter from passersby. Yet somehow, the world felt reduced to this corner, to the two of us and the aroma of strong coffee rising in curls of steam.

Mira tapped her notebook absentmindedly, the ink still fresh from her tick mark. Her eyes gleamed with the kind of contentment that was deeper than just the taste of coffee.

"So," I said, breaking the silence, "what else is on that list of yours?"

She looked at me, feigning suspicion. “Why do you want to know?”

“Because I’m nosy,” I said. Then, softer: “And because I care.”

Her expression softened. She flipped open the notebook, running her fingers over the pages, each line of handwriting uneven yet full of intention. “It’s silly,” she said.

“Let me be the judge.”

She laughed quietly, then began to read.

“Visit Hampi and sketch the ruins,” she began.

“Visit Mysuru”

“Learn how to bake bread properly, not just buy it.”

“Watch the sunrise from Nandi Hills, but only if I wake up before five.”

“Write something worth keeping even if only I keep it.”

Her voice slowed on that last one, her eyes flicking up to gauge my reaction.

I leaned back, sipping the coffee, letting the warmth fill me. “That doesn’t sound silly at all.”

“They’re just… things,” she said, shrugging. “Small things. But they remind me I’m moving forward. That I’m not stuck.”

I thought about my own life. The financial reports stacked on my desk. The schedules, the projections, the endless cycle of weeks that looked identical. My life had no list. Just a loop.

“What else?” I asked.

She hesitated, then smiled mischievously. “Sing karaoke once, even if I embarrass myself.”

I laughed. “That’s ambitious.”

“You’ll come with me,” she said suddenly, as though deciding it on the spot.

I raised an eyebrow. "Will I?"

"Yes," she said firmly. "You don't get a choice. You've already started keeping track of my list you're implicated now."

Her words made me laugh again, but inside, I felt something else: a stirring I couldn't quite name. She was right I *was* implicated. Her life was seeping into mine, her lists folding into my silences.

"You know what's strange?" I said after a pause. "In finance, we make lists too. Except we call them ledgers, projections, budgets. It's all about control, prediction, minimizing surprises. But your list…" I gestured to her notebook. "…your list embraces surprises. It's like an open hand instead of a closed fist."

She tilted her head, intrigued. "And which one do you prefer?"

I thought about it. About my life filled with closed fists squeezing time into measurable returns, holding onto routine so tightly it often left no room for breath. And then I thought about her, about rainstorms that turned into laughter, coffee sipped slowly on a damp night, the way silence felt different when she was in it.

"Yours," I said finally.

Her smile was quiet, but it reached her eyes.

We lingered long after the coffee cooled. She closed her notebook and leaned back, looking up at the night sky where a few hesitant stars had pushed through the city's haze.

"You know what the best part of lists is?" she asked.

"What?"

"Crossing things out. It's proof you lived. That a moment happened. That it wasn't wasted."

I considered that. In finance, we crossed things out too; completed tasks, closed accounts, settled balances. But those never felt like proof of living. Only proof of surviving.

Her way was different. Her list was alive, growing and shrinking, a mirror of her days.

And tonight, I had become part of it.

On the way back, our steps fell into rhythm again, as natural as breathing. She carried her notebook in one hand, her other brushing against the leaves of walls we passed, as though gathering fragments of the night.

"Thank you," she said suddenly.

"For the coffee?" I teased.

"For remembering," she said seriously. "Most people forget. Or they don't notice in the first place. You… notice."

I felt the words settle deep inside me, heavier than they seemed. Nobody had ever told me that before.

We reached my building, and she stopped at the gate. "I should go."

"Good night, Mira."

"Good night, Aditya."

She turned away, her figure fading into the quiet lane. I stood there longer than I needed to, the taste of coffee still lingering on my tongue, her words replaying in my mind.

Back in my flat, the silence felt different. It wasn't empty; it was filled with traces of her laughter, the clink of tumblers, the rustle of notebook pages.

I sat by the window, looking at my plants, wondering if maybe I should make a list too. Not of financial targets, not of deadlines; but of things that made life feel alive.

My pen hovered over a blank page. The first line I wrote was hesitant, almost childish:

*Drink filter coffee with Mira.*

And then I smiled. Because for once, the first box was already ticked.

# To Do List

Two nights later, just as I was rinsing out a coffee cup, the bell rang again. I dried my hands, half-smiling even before I opened the door.

Mira.

This time she didn't look mischievous. She looked… comfortable. As if my doorway was no longer a threshold but a familiar pause.

"Hungry again?" I teased.

She laughed softly. "Always."

And just like that, she stepped in, as though my flat had quietly become an extension of her own.

We found ourselves in the kitchen, chopping vegetables side by side. The space was small enough that our shoulders brushed occasionally, each contact casual yet quietly electric.

She asked, "Did you always cook for yourself?"

"Since college," I said. "Hotel food teaches you survival."

"Survival isn't the same as living," she replied, smiling knowingly.

"You sound like your notebook again."

"Maybe I do." She laughed, scraping diced carrots into the pan. "But tell me, what did you eat at home as a kid?"

The question caught me off guard. I thought of my mother, tired but insistent on making rasam from scratch, the smell of tamarind and curry leaves filling our small kitchen. I thought of my father, strict about meals being on time, though he rarely joined us.

"Rasam," I said softly. "Every week. No matter what. Even when we couldn't agree on anything else."

Her face softened. "I love rasam."

Something about her tone made me ache; a mix of nostalgia and longing, as if rasam was less about food and more about home.

As the food simmered, she leaned against the counter, arms folded.

"My mother still thinks I'll come around to arranged marriage one day," she admitted. "She keeps showing me profiles. Nice boys with stable jobs."

I smirked. "Finance guys?"

She shot me a look. "Some of them, yes." Then, more seriously: "She means well. But I can't imagine… loving like that. Through spreadsheets of compatibility."

Her words struck deeper than she realized. My entire career was built on spreadsheets, on numbers, ratios, probability. But here she was, refusing to reduce love to an equation.

"What about your family?" she asked.

"My father believes marriage is stability," I said slowly. "My mother… she never argued, but I could see she didn't agree. She wanted me to choose. To wait until it felt right."

"And do you think it ever will?"

I didn't answer immediately. The pan hissed behind us, filling the silence with spice and heat. Finally, I said, "Maybe it already has. I just don't know what to call it yet."

She looked at me, startled. But before either of us could add more, the timer beeped. The spell broke.

We ate on the balcony this time, plates balanced on our laps, the night breeze carrying faint city sounds. Mira tasted the curry and groaned with exaggerated delight.

"Aditya, this is dangerously good. You're ruining my expectations of bachelor's forever."

"Good," I said. "Lower expectations lead to fewer disappointments."

She laughed so hard she nearly spilled her plate. And in that laughter, the heaviness of our earlier conversation softened, reshaped into something gentler.

After dinner, she pulled out her notebook again. The cover was worn now, the corners bent, pages crowded with handwriting.

"I added new things," she said, flipping it open.

"Let's hear them."

"Take a night bus to Pondicherry. Learn to swim properly. Plant a tree that I'll visit years later. And…" She hesitated, tapping her pen against the page. "…teach someone something they'll never forget."

I leaned closer. "That last one's big."

She shrugged. "Maybe. But big things start small."

"Like filter coffee," I said.

She grinned. "Exactly."

Then, almost shyly, she asked, "Did you ever start your own list?"

I froze. She had noticed.

Slowly, I reached for a notebook from my desk a plain black one, nothing like her worn, lived-in book. I flipped it open to the first page.

Only one line sat there, in my neat handwriting: *Drink filter coffee with Mira.*

Her eyes widened. "You did."

"And I ticked it," I said quietly.

She smiled. No, she beamed. "Aditya, that's… that's perfect."

For a moment, we sat in silence, our two notebooks open on the table between us, like two lives slowly intertwining.

The evening stretched on. We talked about books, about music we used to love, about the strange loneliness of being surrounded by people in a city that never slept.

At some point, I realized the way she sat legs tucked beneath her, leaning slightly toward me. The distance between us had shrunk, not through intention but through comfort.

And I thought this is how love begins. Not with grand gestures, but with vegetables chopped side by side, with rasam remembered, with notebooks shared across a quiet table.

As the evening stretched toward night, Mira closed her notebook, holding it against her chest. Her smile was lighter now, but there was a shadow beneath it, a weight I recognized.

"You're still waiting, aren't you?" I asked.

She nodded. "They said a week. It's been four days. Every time my phone buzzes, I hope it's them. Every time it isn't, I feel…" She trailed off, searching for the word. "…smaller."

I wanted to tell her she wasn't small, that no company's decision could ever measure her worth. But in this world, the world of interviews and approvals, offers and rejections, words like that always risked sounding empty.

So, I simply said, "They'd be lucky to have you."

She looked at me, her eyes softening. "Do you really think so?"

"I know so."

She exhaled, as though releasing a knot she'd been holding all day.

Later, when the dishes were washed and the night deepened, I asked, “Coffee?”

Her eyes lit up. “Again?”

I smiled. “Always.”

We stepped out into the cool air, the streets quieter now, their dampness carrying the leftover scent of rain. The filter coffee stall was still open, brass tumblers stacked high, steam curling into the night.

We stood side by side as the vendor poured the hot, frothy coffee back and forth between tumblers, the rhythm hypnotic. Mira leaned closer and whispered, “Every time I come here, I feel like I’m tasting the city itself.”

“And now you can tick it again,” I said.

She grinned. “If I start ticking the same things twice, my list will never end.”

“Maybe that’s the point,” I replied.

We found a bench nearby, tumblers warming our hands once again. Mira opened her notebook, flipping to the same page where she had checked off *filter coffee*. She tapped the corner thoughtfully.

“Do you know Aditya, even in 2019, I prefer to write in a notebook than in mobile.”

“You know what’s funny?” she asked.

“What?”

“I started this list to keep myself moving, to remind myself I wasn’t stuck. But lately…” She hesitated, her eyes meeting mine. “…lately, the things I want to do aren’t just mine anymore. They’re ours.”

Her voice was quiet, but the word *ours* reverberated in me like a struck chord.

I thought of my own blank notebook, of the single line I had written and ticked. I thought of how empty it looked compared to hers but also how it felt less like a beginning and more like a bridge.

"Then maybe," I said softly, "we should start a new list. Together."

She looked at me for a long time, the steam from her coffee curling between us. Then she smiled slow, certain, luminous.

"Maybe we should."

She didn't write anything down then. Neither did I. But something unspoken passed between us, something more binding than ink.

The world around us carried on autos rattling past, a stray dog nosing through wrappers, the vendor clinking coins into a tin box. But for me, the world had narrowed to this: Mira, her smile, the glow of a streetlight reflecting in her eyes.

On the walk back, she said suddenly, "You know… if I don't get that job, I'll not be disappointed neither I won't feel lost."

"Why not?" I asked.

"Because some things matter more than an offer letter," she said simply. Then, almost shyly: "Like this. Like tonight."

I didn't reply. Words felt unnecessary. Instead, I let the silence stretch, filled with the rhythm of our footsteps, the soft hum of the city.

When we reached my flat, she lingered at the gate.

"Good night, Aditya," she said, her voice warm, steady.

"Good night, Mira."

She smiled, then added, "Don't forget you promised we'd start a list together."

"I won't," I said.

And as I watched her walk away, notebook tucked close, I realized something undeniable: The waiting for her confirmation, for answers, for whatever came next no longer frightened me.

Because waiting, with her in my world, had begun to feel less like emptiness, and more like promise.

# The Good News

It started, as these things often do, with whispers. I was bent over my desk, staring at an excel sheet where numbers had begun to blur into each other, when two colleagues from HR walked past, voices low but hurried. I wasn't paying attention until I heard one of them say:

"…yes, that writer girl, Mira, she's confirmed. Offer letter cleared."

I'm happy.

For a moment, I wasn't sure if I had really heard her name, or if my tired mind was playing tricks on me. But then another voice chimed in:

"Good find for communications, we needed someone sharp. She'll fit in."

And just like that, the world tilted.

Mira.
Selected.
Here.

I leaned back in my chair, heart hammering in a way it never did during market crashes or late-night deadlines. My fingers hovered uselessly over the keyboard, unable to process another formula.

She had done it. She had made it through.

The image of her sitting nervously in the lobby a few days ago flashed back to me. The way she had tapped her notebook, whispered she wasn't sure she could handle it. I had told her she'd be fine and now, she was.

I should have returned to my work, but instead, a reel of images began unspooling in my head.

Mira, walking through these very office halls with her notebook tucked under her arm. Mira, sitting across the cafeteria table at lunch, mocking me for how seriously I ate my curd rice. Mira, waiting at the lift as the morning crowd jostled around us, her eyes rolling at the chaos but her smile steady.

The thought that we could now share not only evenings but entire days, it was overwhelming.

I pictured us on the metro together every morning. She'd tease me about my habit of counting stations, and I'd remind her to carry an umbrella because Bangalore skies were never trustworthy. We'd carve out a corner of routine together, an orbit within the city's chaos.

And in the evenings, instead of parting ways at the fork, we could walk home side by side, carrying the weight of the same day, the same stories.

The fantasy unfurled effortlessly, like it had been waiting in some quiet corner of my mind all along.

That evening, as I boarded the metro at Baiyappanahalli, the city looked brighter, softer. Even the metallic clang of the arriving train felt less jarring, almost musical.

I found a seat by the window and let myself drift. Outside, the city whirred by in blurred streaks of neon and concrete. Inside, my mind wandered into futures not yet lived.

I imagined her sitting beside me, notebook balanced on her knees, scribbling down an idea between stations. I'd watch the way her pen moved, the way her forehead furrowed slightly when she concentrated.

At Swami Vivekananda Road, I pictured her laughing at something Pranav might say if he suddenly burst into our coach with his endless jokes. At Halasuru, I saw her leaning against the glass, watching the Ulsoor Lake shimmer in the fading light. By the time the train rolled past Trinity, I was smiling like a fool, lost in dreams too vivid to resist.

It wasn't just the thought of her joining the office. It was the idea of her weaving into the fabric of my days, turning ordinary commutes and cafeteria lunches into something memorable.

I realized, with a jolt, that I wasn't just happy for her success. I was selfishly happy for what it meant for *me*. For us.

When the train reached MG Road, I almost hated to leave it. The ride had been too full of sweet, impossible possibilities.

I took an auto back to my flat, the driver weaving through traffic while I sat in the back, still wrapped in daydreams. By the time we turned into my lane, I felt a lightness in my chest I hadn't felt in years.

I climbed the stairs to my apartment, rehearsing in my head how I'd congratulate her. Maybe I'd pretend I didn't know, let her tell me first. Or maybe I'd blurt it out, unable to contain myself. Either way, tonight would be different.

I set my bag down, loosened my tie, still smiling. And then just as if the universe had timed it perfectly the doorbell rang.

I knew before I opened it. Somehow, I knew.

I swung the door wide, enthusiasm rushing ahead of me like a flood.

"Mira."

She stood there, framed in the soft glow of the corridor light, her face brighter than I had ever seen it. Not just happy, radiant. There was something about her expression that made the air between us spark with possibility.

"You look… bright today," I said, unable to hide my grin.

She smiled back, her eyes dancing. "I have news."

My heart thudded. *I know,* I thought. *I already know.*

But I didn't say it. I wanted to hear it from her lips, to let her unwrap the moment herself.

"One good news," she continued, "and one bad news."

The smile faltered slightly on my lips, though I tried to keep it steady. Good news and bad news. This wasn't how I had scripted it in my head on the metro.

Still, I forced a light tone. "Then tell me the bad news first." Because I know the good news is she got selected.

Her eyes flickered with something unreadable. And in that flicker, I realized my dreams from the metro ride might not unfold the way I had imagined.

I leaned against the doorframe, trying to keep my voice casual. "Alright then, let's hear the bad news first."

She smiled faintly, as though amused by my choice. Then she said it with disarming simplicity:

"I got the job in your company. But I'm not joining."

For a moment, I just stared. Her words didn't make sense. The first half sounded like triumph; the kind of sentence I had been waiting to hear all day. But the second half knocked the air out of me.

"You're… not joining?"

She shook her head gently. "No."

Something heavy settled in my chest. All the little dreams I had built on the metro, her by my side on the morning ride, her at the cafeteria, her laughter in the same corridors, all of them scattered like paper in a sudden wind.

"But why?" I asked finally, my voice sharper than I intended. "If you got the offer, why wouldn't you?"

She lifted her hand, stopping me. "It lies in the good news."

I stepped back, letting her into the flat. She walked in, setting her notebook on the coffee table, and turned toward me with that calmness I both admired and resented in moments like this.

"You're angry," she said softly.

"I'm not angry," I lied. "I'm… confused."

Her eyes searched mine, and I knew she could see more than I wanted to reveal. My excitement, my hope, it had been too obvious.

"Aditya," she said gently, "you'll understand once I tell you the good news."

But she didn't say it immediately. Instead, she wandered toward the shelf with my plants, touching the leaves of the jade plant like she had the first time she entered. The silence between us thickened.

I realized how deeply I had let myself imagine things, how far ahead I had run in a matter of hours. And now, standing in my own living room, she was unravelling it with one quiet sentence.

"Are you hungry?" I asked, my tone heavier than I intended.

She nodded. "Starving."

"Let's cook, then," I muttered, heading into the kitchen.

She followed, as always. But this time, the kitchen didn't feel intimate. It felt like a stage where an unspoken argument was unfolding.

I set a pan on the stove, poured oil, chopped onions with more force than necessary. She noticed, of course.

"You're upset," she said quietly, handing me the green chilies.

"I'm not upset," I repeated, though my hands betrayed me, moving too fast, knife striking the board with sharp thuds.

"Yes, you are." She didn't push further, just watched me.

And in her silence, I heard everything: her certainty, her patience, her refusal to be rushed into telling me what I wanted to know.

The onions hissed in the pan. The smell filled the small kitchen, but it didn't soothe me the way it usually did. I kept my eyes on the stove, unwilling to meet hers.

"You know," I said finally, "on the metro today, I was thinking about us traveling together. Every morning. Every evening. It felt… possible. Real."

Her breath caught, but she said nothing.

"And now," I added, lowering the flame, "you tell me you're not joining. Do you know what that feels like?"

There was a pause. Then, gently, she said, "It feels like disappointment. I know. And I'm sorry."

I turned then, finally meeting her eyes. She wasn't defensive. She wasn't dismissive. She looked almost pained like my hurt was her own.

And in that moment, I realized something: whatever the good news was, it wasn't going to heal the sting of the bad. It was going to change the shape of it, perhaps even deepen it.

We finished the cooking in silence, each lost in separate thoughts. The rhythm we had built in this kitchen over the last few evenings felt broken, replaced by something tentative.

As the curry simmered, she finally spoke.

"Aditya," she said softly, "will you let me tell you the good news now?"

I swallowed hard. My throat felt dry, as though I had been bracing for a blow I couldn't avoid.

"Tell me," I said.

She nodded slowly; her expression unreadable. "But first, sit. I don't want to tell you standing over onions."

We moved back to the living room. She sat on the couch, pillow in her lap. I sat across, hands clasped tightly.

Her fingers traced the edge of the pillow before she looked up.

"The good news," she said, "is that I got another offer. A better one. In Mumbai." I'm going back.

# Not the Good News

Her words landed like a stone dropped into still water: *Mumbai.* For a moment, I wasn't sure I had heard right.

"You're moving to Mumbai?" I asked slowly.

"Yes."

She said it with a steadiness that both reassured and unsettled me.

"Why didn't you tell me that was your hometown?"

A faint smile tugged at her lips. "You never asked. And… I never felt the need to mention it. Bangalore was our story, not Mumbai."

Our story. The words flickered inside me, half-comfort, half-cut.

She continued, her voice calmer than my racing thoughts. "The offer is stronger, better role, better pay, a chance to actually lead projects instead of just assisting. And…" She hesitated, lowering her gaze. "…my parents are there. I haven't lived at home in years. Maybe it's time."

I sat back, struggling to piece it together. A better job, family, home everything she said made sense. Too much sense.

And yet, all I could feel was the unraveling of the dream I had built on my metro ride home.

"So," I said, forcing the words through the knot in my throat, "you won't be here."

She shook her head gently. "Not for long. Two more months. Then… Mumbai."

The casualness with which she said it struck me like cold water. Two months. Just sixty days. A fraction of time, barely enough to catch my breath, let alone adjust to the idea of losing the rhythm we had only just begun to build.

"Aditya…" She leaned forward, searching my face. "Say something."

"What do you want me to say?" The bitterness slipped out before I could stop it. "Congratulations? That I'm happy for you?"

She flinched. Not dramatically, but enough for me to notice.

"I don't need your congratulations," she said softly. "I just need you to understand."

The food on the stove demanded attention, so we drifted back to the kitchen. This time, there was no easy laughter, no playful teasing over salt and spice. Only silence, thick and heavy.

I stirred the curry mechanically while she sliced cucumbers, each slice falling into the bowl with soft thuds that seemed louder than they should.

My mind kept looping: her in Mumbai, me here. The metro rides I had imagined, erased. The coffee stalls, the late-night lists, all slowly dissolving into a countdown I couldn't stop.

"You're quiet," she said gently.

I didn't look up. "What do you want me to say, Mira? That I'm okay with it?"

Her knife paused mid-slice. "I want you to be honest."

I turned then, finally meeting her eyes. "Honestly? I don't want you to go."

The silence that followed was not heavy it was raw.

She put the knife down, folding her arms across her chest. "Aditya… my whole life isn't here. It never was. I love what we've found, these evenings, these lists, this… us. But I can't build my career on borrowed ground. Mumbai is where I can grow. Where my family is. Where…" She broke off, searching for words. "…where I feel like I belong."

Her honesty was brutal in its clarity. She wasn't choosing against me; she was choosing for herself. And yet, it felt the same.

"Do you understand?" she asked softly.

I nodded stiffly. "I understand. Doesn't mean I like it."

Her lips curved into a sad smile. "That's fair."

We ate in near silence, the clink of spoons louder than any words. The curry tasted fine, but every bite felt like a negotiation with disappointment.

At one point, she looked at me and said, "You'll still walk with me, won't you? Until I leave?"

I swallowed hard. "Of course."

And I meant it. Even if each step would carry the weight of a ticking clock, I couldn't imagine giving them up.

After dinner, she wandered back to the couch, notebook in hand. She didn't open it this time. She just held it, as though the act of holding was enough.

"I've added Mumbai to my list," she said finally. "Not just as a job. As… a return. As a chapter I need to write."

I nodded, though my heart felt heavier than ever.

She looked at me then, her eyes softer. "That doesn't erase this chapter, Aditya. You're in it. More than you know."

And though I wanted to believe her, all I could think about was how fragile words feel when measured against the certainty of distance.

After we cleared the plates and left the kitchen in order, Mira asked softly, "Can we walk a little? Just around the lane?"

It was the kind of request she often made, but tonight it carried a different weight. We stepped out into the night air. The streets were damp again, traces of the afternoon rain still lingering in small puddles that caught the glow of the streetlamps. The world smelled faintly of wet earth, diesel, and the subtle sweetness of jasmine from someone's balcony. For a few steps, neither of us spoke. Our footsteps echoed quietly, like two parallel lines tracing the same path but never quite meeting.

Normally our walks carried laughter, teasing, the low hum of easy conversation. Tonight, silence walked with us. But it wasn't an empty silence—it was full of things unsaid, heavy and humming.

I kept thinking about two months.

Two months to turn into memories.

Two months before she was gone.

And yet, as I glanced sideways at her, watching her tuck a strand of hair behind her ear, I thought *better two months than none.*

"Aditya," she said softly, eyes fixed ahead, "I know this is hard to hear. I know it isn't what you wanted. But I need you to know something."

I looked at her, waiting.

"These walks… they've been the best part of my days. I don't want them to stop. Not until I leave. Maybe not even after, if I can carry them with me."

Her voice trembled slightly on that last line. She wasn't as composed as she had seemed earlier. Beneath the confidence about Mumbai, there was hesitation too, a sadness that mirrored my own.

"I kept imagining," I admitted quietly, "you and me on the metro. At the office. Living the same days together. It felt… possible."

She smiled sadly. "And now it doesn't."

"No. Now it doesn't."

We walked a little further, passing under the branches of a Gul mohar tree, its flowers scattered on the pavement like red embers. The sight felt symbolic beauty scattered because it couldn't hold on.

"Two months," I said. "That's all we have."

"That's not nothing," she replied gently. "That's sixty evenings. Sixty walks. Sixty cups of coffee if we want. Sixty more chances to add to our lists."

I stopped, looking at her. The streetlamp lit her face in fragments—shadow on one side, gold on the other.

"Do you really think lists can hold back time?" I asked.

She held my gaze steadily. "Not hold it back. But hold it *in.*"

Her words lingered in the air, and I realized she was right. We couldn't stop what was coming, but we could shape how it would live inside us.

She pulled her mobile from her pocket. On a notes, she typed quickly, then showed me:

*Make the most of sixty days.*

I stared at the words. Then, without thinking, I opened a note in mobile. I typed the same line.

Two things. One line.

"This is what we meant of having the same to do list?" I asked

She smiled, closing hers with a snap. "Now it became."

We turned back toward my flat. The night was cooler now, a soft breeze carrying the faint sound of distant traffic. Mira walked close, not touching, but close enough that her presence was undeniable.

At the gate, she paused. "Good night, Aditya."

"Good night."

She hesitated, then added, "Thank you… for not shutting down. For still walking with me."

I nodded, unable to trust my voice.

Back in my room, the silence pressed in. I sat at my desk, looking at the line I had typed: *Make the most of sixty days.* For the first time, my list felt urgent, almost desperate.

I thought of all the things we could still do coffee shops unexplored, parks unwandered, conversations unspoken. I thought of her laughter, her notebook, the way she touched my plants as if they were alive in ways I had never noticed.

And I realized something: love wasn't about permanence. It was about presence.

If all I had was sixty days, then I would live them. All of them. With her.

I lay in bed, listening to the faint hum of the city. Somewhere, a dog barked; somewhere else, a bike roared down an empty road. But inside me, there was only the echo of her voice:

*Not hold time back. Hold it in.*

I closed my eyes, clutching the pillow to my chest. For once, the future didn't matter. Only tomorrow did.

Only the next walk.

# The Ring

The morning broke softer than usual. The city, still shaking off its night's dampness, smelled faintly of wet soil and early jasmine. When I stepped out of my flat, half expecting the usual solitude of the lane, I found Mira already standing near the Gul mohar tree, waiting. It's been a week since she told that she is leaving to Mumbai.

Her notebook wasn't in her hand this time. She just stood there, adjusting her dupatta against the breeze, eyes fixed somewhere ahead, as if she were already walking through a future I couldn't see.

"You're early," I said.

She turned, her smile carrying that familiar brightness that made the ordinary seem remarkable. "So are you."

We fell into step together, the way we always did, our rhythm found almost without effort.

We started towards Metro station, where the road split toward the metro station, I finally gathered the nerve.

"Mira," I said.

"Yes?"

"Can I… have your number?"

For a fraction of a second, her brow lifted in surprise, as though amused by the sudden formality of my request. Then she smiled, tilting her head playfully.

"You took long enough."

I fumbled for my phone, and she dictated it slowly, each digit sinking into my memory as though carved there. When her name appeared on my screen, saved and certain, I felt an inexplicable relief, as if I had secured proof that she existed beyond our lanes and our walks.

"Now you can bother me even when I'm not standing next to you," she teased.

"Don't tempt me," I said.

We reached the MG Road station, climbing the stairs together into the rush of the morning. The trains hissed and hummed, doors opening to swallow the crowd.

We boarded the same coach, and for once, the jostling didn't bother me. Mira stood near the door, holding the railing, while I found a spot beside her. The train pulled away, its windows opening to the city unraveling below, the tangle of roads, the steady stream of autos, the rooftops still glistening from last night's rain.

For three stations, we shared that space, the occasional brush of her sleeve against mine, her soft laughter when she pointed out a child on the platform waving to the train as if it were alive.

At Trinity, she glanced at me. "I change at Halasuru. My office is that way."

I nodded, pretending to be casual. But the thought of her peeling away from my line left a hollowness I hadn't anticipated.

At Halasuru, as the doors opened, she stepped out. She turned back briefly, lifting her hand in a small wave.

"See you in the evening?" she asked.

"Of course."

And then she was gone, swept into the crowd, while the doors closed and carried me onward toward Baiyappanahalli.

The rest of the ride felt strange emptier without her, but fuller with the thought that now, if I wanted, I could reach her. A message, a call, a fragment of connection waiting in my pocket.

I stared at her name glowing on my phone screen and felt a rush of something dangerously close to happiness.

In a city of millions, she had become the one constant thread weaving through my days. And now, with her number saved, that thread no longer felt fragile.

By the time I stepped off at Baiyappanahalli, I was already lost in imagination again.

What if, one morning, we boarded together and never split directions? What if her office wasn't at Halasuru but beside mine? What if evenings weren't just Gul mohar walks but dinners, movies, shared routines?

The fantasies unfolded recklessly, unchecked, filling the gaps between traffic horns and office deadlines. For the first time in years, my day at work felt almost light not because the numbers had changed, but because something within me had.

That night, as I sat by the window, plants casting shadows on the wall, I scrolled to her name on my phone again. I didn't message her. Not yet.

It was enough, for now, to know that I could.

The next day unfolded in the familiar monotony of numbers and meetings, but beneath the surface, my mind was elsewhere. Mira's number sat in my phone like a secret burning to be used, and every so often, I'd unlock the screen just to see it, to remind myself it was real.

But more than the digits, it was the thought that pressed in on me: *Tell her.*

The words looped through my head like a mantra. Tell her before time runs out. Tell her before Mumbai pulls her away. Tell her, because hesitation had already cost me too much in life.

By afternoon, the decision was made. Tonight, I would ask her to dinner. Tonight, I would tell her.

I drafted the text three times before settling on the simplest version:

*Dinner tonight? Just us.*

I stared at it for a full minute, then hit send before I could lose courage.

Her reply came sooner than expected:

*Sure. Where?*

My heart jumped. I named a small restaurant I liked quiet, warm, tucked away from the chaos of MG Road. A place where confessions might feel less intimidating.

*Perfect,* she wrote back.

It was settled.

But something restless stirred in me. Words felt too fragile, too fleeting. I wanted something to anchor what I was about to say, something tangible she could hold.

So, after office, I walked into a store. The glass counters gleamed under soft lights, rows of silver and gold whispering promises of permanence.

A saleswoman approached. "Looking for something specific, sir?"

I hesitated, then said, "Something simple. Not flashy. But… meaningful."

She nodded knowingly and pulled out a delicate silver ring shaped like the infinity symbol. Subtle, elegant, unpretentious yet carrying a promise larger than itself.

When I slipped it onto my palm, it caught the light in a quiet shimmer.

"This one," I said.

I walked out of the store with the small box tucked into my pocket, my fingers brushing against it as if to reassure myself it was still there.

Back home, I stood before the mirror, rehearsing in silence.

How do you say it?

*Mira, I love you.* Too blunt.

*Mira, these months have changed me.* Too vague.

*Mira, will you...* No. Not yet.

I laughed at myself, shaking my head. There was no perfect script. There was only honesty.

I slid the ring box into my jacket pocket and checked it twice before leaving. My heart thudded with each step down the stairs, each turn toward the restaurant.

Then my phone buzzed. A message from Mira:

*I'll come directly to the restaurant. Don't wait at the lane.*

I typed back quickly: *Okay.*

Relief mingled with nerves. Soon. Very soon.

The restaurant glowed softly under warm lights. I chose a table by the corner, one that offered both privacy and a view of the street outside. I ordered water, checked my watch, then checked the ring box again.

Every tick of the second hand was a countdown. My palms felt clammy. My mind played through every possible scenario, her surprise, her smile, her laughter, maybe even her tears.

Ten minutes later, the door opened. Mira walked in bright, radiant, her presence pulling the air toward her.

But she wasn't alone.

Beside her was another woman, tall, graceful, carrying an easy confidence that matched Mira's smile.

Mira waved when she spotted me. "Aditya!"

My heart sank even before she reached the table.

# A Trip

Mira reached the table with her usual brightness. “Aditya, this is Ramya,” she said, gesturing to the woman beside her.

Ramya smiled warmly, extending a hand. “So, you’re the Aditya I’ve been hearing about.”

I shook her hand, my own smile practiced but strained. “Good to meet you.”

Inside, my carefully prepared script the words, the courage, the box in my pocket crumbled into silence.

“Hope you don’t mind me joining,” Ramya said as she sat down. “Mira and I made plans earlier, and then she said you’d invited her for dinner. I thought, why not all together?”

I forced a nod. “Of course. The more, the merrier.”

But the words tasted hollow.

Throughout the meal, I played the part of the polite host. I smiled at Ramya’s stories, laughed at Mira’s jokes, asked questions when silence threatened. But beneath it all, the ring box pressed against my side, a constant reminder of what I wasn’t saying.

At one point, Mira leaned forward, eyes sparkling. “Aditya, did you know Ramya’s a photographer? She’s been documenting old neighborhoods before they vanish under new construction.”

“That’s incredible,” I said sincerely. And it was. But even as Ramya described her work, all I could think about was the infinity ring hidden just inches from Mira’s hand.

It was supposed to be tonight. It was supposed to be us.

Dinner stretched on, dishes arriving, conversations flowing. To an outsider, we must have looked like friends enjoying a pleasant evening. But inside me, a storm raged a blend of hope, frustration, and the sharp ache of missed timing.

I watched Mira laugh at something Ramya said, her eyes crinkling at the edges, and thought: *This could have been the moment I told you. This could have been the night you knew.*

But I said nothing.

When the bill came, I reached for it automatically, but Ramya insisted on splitting. Mira teased us both about being stubborn, her laughter lightening the tension at the table.

And still, I said nothing.

As we stepped out of the restaurant into the cool night, the city buzzing faintly around us, my hand brushed the ring box once more. Its weight felt unbearable now, no longer a promise but a secret.

I slipped it deeper into my pocket, where it would remain unseen.

At the corner where we were to part, Ramya hailed an auto. Mira hugged her goodbye, promising to call tomorrow. Then she turned to me, her expression softer now, almost apologetic.

"Thanks for dinner," she said. "It was good, wasn't it?"

I managed a smile. "It was."

She looked at me for a moment longer, as though sensing the unspoken words I carried. But she didn't ask. And I didn't tell.

"Good night, Aditya."

"Good night, Mira."

She walked away; her silhouette swallowed by the crowd.

Back in my flat, I placed the ring box on the table, staring at it under the dim lamp. The infinity symbol shimmered faintly, mocking me with its irony. Infinite possibilities and yet, here I was, silenced by hesitation and circumstance.

I slipped the box back into a drawer, shutting it away. Not discarded but not given either. Suspended.

And with it, my confession remained suspended too.

I was still staring at the closed drawer, the ring hidden inside, when my phone buzzed. It was Mira.

*Aditya, quick update. We're going to Mysuru tomorrow. An immediate plan. Ramya and I thought of it just now.*

I blinked, rereading the lines. Immediate plan. Tomorrow.

Another message followed almost instantly:

*I might not come back to Bangalore before I move to Mumbai. So... this could be my last trip from here. Will you come with us?*

My heart lurched. She was inviting me in, offering one more space to share, maybe even one last.

And yet something inside me recoiled.

My fingers hovered over the keyboard. I typed slowly, deliberately, as though the words would matter less if I pretended, they weren't heavy.

*I can't. I have an important meeting tomorrow.*

The lie sent a chill through me even as I hit send.

Her reply came quickly:

*I understand. We'll click photos and I'll show you later.*

There was no disappointment in her words. But I felt it anyway.

The next day, I woke earlier than usual. The city outside was just beginning to stretch awake, skies still pale.

There was no meeting. No schedule. No urgency waiting at my desk.

Just silence.

I made coffee, sat by the window, and let the truth settle: I had refused. Again.

I could have been on the train with her now, heading toward Mysuru, watching the landscape unfurl into green fields and distant hills. I could have been beside her, listening to her stories, her laughter echoing in compartments filled with strangers.

Instead, I was here, alone, staring at the steam rising from a cup that tasted bitter.

Why hadn't I gone?

The question circled endlessly in my head. Fear, perhaps. Not fear of her, but of myself of what her presence stirred in me, of the possibility of confessing and being met with silence, or worse, pity.

So, I had chosen safety. Distance. A meeting that didn't exist.

And yet, the irony cut deeper: I was losing her anyway. Mumbai loomed like an inevitability. My silence wasn't protecting me it was erasing me.

I opened the drawer and took out the ring box. The infinity symbol glimmered faintly in the morning light.

It should have been on her hand by now, warm against her skin, a promise made tangible. Instead, it was a reminder of everything unsaid.

I closed the box again, pressing it to my forehead briefly, as though it could absorb the ache in me.

I had not lost Mira because of Mumbai, or because of jobs, or because of time. I was losing her because of hesitation my own.

And unless something changed, hesitation would keep winning.

# The Unsaid

The morning Mira left for Mysuru was quieter than usual. She had texted me before sunrise:

*Boarding the train now. Will send you photos later. Take care, Aditya.*

I read the message twice, the words too casual, too light for the weight they carried. This wasn't just a trip; it was a rehearsal of absence.

I typed a reply *Have a Safe travel. Enjoy.* Then deleted it. Then typed it again.
And finally sent it, though the words felt inadequate.

And just like that, she was gone. For three days.

Evening, when I stepped out for my usual walk, the Gul mohar tree stood where it always did, but without Mira beside it, it looked less like a landmark and more like a reminder.

Children still played cricket in the lanes, shouting with the same reckless joy. Couples still strolled; heads bent together in private conversations. The bougainvillea still spilled over walls in bursts of pink and purple.

But the world felt thinner, as if a layer had been peeled away.

I walked slowly, deliberately, but it wasn't the same. The rhythm we had built, the unspoken coordination of our steps, the way her notebook sometimes slipped under her arm all of it was missing.

Every corner carried her absence.

Back home, I stared at her name glowing on my phone.

I wanted to text: *How's Mysuru?*

Or: *Don't forget the Mysore pak, mylari dosa there!.*

Or simply: *I miss you.*

But I didn't.

Instead, I placed the phone face down, as though that could silence the ache.

Because in my mind, a cruel thought repeated: *If love is unsaid, maybe this is what it looks like. Empty lanes. Silent phones. Walks alone.*

That night stretched endlessly. I cooked for myself, but the food tasted bland. I opened a book, but the words swam uselessly. Even music, which usually shielded me, felt hollow.

I found myself pacing by the window, staring at the plants she had once touched with such care, remembering how she laughed at my careful watering schedule.

The room felt too clean, too quiet, as if waiting for a presence that wouldn't come.

It struck me then that my restraint wasn't noble, it was fear. Fear of appearing desperate, fear of admitting to myself what I already knew.

Because to text her would be to acknowledge the depth of what I felt. And if she didn't respond with the same depth? I didn't know if I could bear it.

So, I chose silence.

And silence, I realized, was another word for cowardice.

As I finally lay down, the city's night noises filling the air, distant horns, a barking dog, the hum of a ceiling fan, I whispered into the dark:

"If love stays unsaid, it will stay like this forever."

And the thought chilled me more than the night air ever could.

The second day passed slowly, dragging its feet like a reluctant child. At the office, I buried myself in work, crunching numbers with unusual vigor, pretending deadlines were urgent. My colleagues assumed I was being productive; in truth, I was running.

Every time my phone buzzed; my heart jumped. But it was always work emails, meeting reminders, or pointless promotional messages. No Mira.

I told myself she was busy exploring Mysuru wandering through markets, scribbling in her notebook, photographing palaces and streets. The thought of her immersed in life gave me comfort, even as her absence gnawed at me.

That evening, I walked the familiar lane again. The Gul mohar tree loomed like an unlit lamp present but lifeless. Without her beside me, I felt like a solitary shadow pretending to be whole.

By the third day, the emptiness had grown sharper. I found myself replaying her voice in my head the way she said "Aditya" with a mix of teasing and seriousness, the pauses she left between thoughts, the warmth hidden in her laughter.

I sat by my plants that evening, touching the leaves as she had once done, hearing her echo: *"Not everyone remembers to water them."*

I smiled despite myself, then felt the smile fade. Memory was a poor substitute for presence.

That night, I dreamed of the metro. I dreamed she was beside me, holding the railing, her reflection caught in the window. But when I turned to speak, she was gone, leaving only an empty seat.

I woke up with my chest tight, the dream's absence heavier than reality.

On the fourth day, I gave in and scrolled through our message thread. It was sparse, just small confirmations of dinner plans, reminders, brief exchanges. No confessions. No depth.

I typed a message: *How's Mysuru?* My thumb hovered over send.

Then I deleted it.

I told myself: *If she wanted to tell me, she would.*

But the truth was harsher: *If I wanted to know, I should ask.*

Instead, I chose silence again, watching the day pass like sand slipping through fingers.

That night, unable to sleep, I argued with myself.

*Why don't you just tell her?*

Because what if she doesn't feel the same?

*And what if she does?*

Then Mumbai still takes her away. *So, isn't it better to know than wonder forever?*

But knowing means risking the peace of what we have now.

Round and round, the voices circled, until exhaustion silenced them.

Loneliness, I realized, was a cruel but honest mirror. In her absence, I could no longer hide behind daily rituals or shared laughter. I saw myself clearly: a man who let hesitation write his story.

If I stayed this way, the ending was obvious. She would leave for Mumbai, carrying her lists and her laughter, while I remained here, clutching a ring in a drawer and a silence in my chest.

And the thought of that ending terrified me more than rejection ever could.

I stood at the window watching the city lights flicker, I whispered aloud:

"This can't be how it ends. Not unsaid. Not like this."

The words felt like a promise not to her yet, but to me.

On the fifth evening, as I stepped out of my flat for yet another hollow walk, I saw her.

Mira, standing under the Gul mohar tree as if the three days apart had been nothing but a brief pause. She wore a pale blue kurta, her hair loose, her smile easy and unguarded.

For a moment, I froze. The lane, the tree, even the noise of children playing nearby, all blurred into insignificance. Only she was clear.

She looked up, saw me, and waved. “Aditya.”

Her voice cut through the emptiness of the past three nights, and I felt something in me unclench.

Walking toward her, I became acutely aware of the difference.

The past four evenings had been filled with silence, shadows, and self-doubt. Tonight, her presence shifted everything. The air felt lighter, the colors sharper, the world less indifferent.

It was almost unfair, how much power her presence carried.

“You’re back,” I said, trying to keep my voice steady.

“Of course,” she replied. “Did you miss me?”

The question was playful, but it caught me off guard. My instinct was to say yes, to admit how empty the days had been. Instead, I smiled weakly and said, “The lane was quieter.”

She laughed, shaking her head. “That’s your way of saying yes.”

As we walked, she launched into stories from her trip.

“The palace was breathtaking at dusk like a painting catching fire,” she said, her hands gesturing as if to sketch it in the air. “And the market! So many colors, so much noise, I bought a scarf, I’ll show you sometime.”

Her words tumbled out with excitement; her voice alive with the rhythm of travel. She described the food, Mysore pak, the people, the narrow lanes she had wandered with Ramya, the temple bells ringing at dawn.

I listened, smiling, but beneath it all, I felt the ache of those three days more keenly. She had lived so fully while I had merely endured.

At one point, she stopped mid-story and looked at me. "You're quiet tonight."

I hesitated. "I was just… listening."

She tilted her head. "Or thinking?"

Both, I wanted to say. Thinking of how much I missed you. Thinking of how easily silence turns into regret. Thinking of how close I am to telling you everything.

But I swallowed the words, letting them dissolve into the night.

We reached the small park where we often sat. Mira leaned against the bench; her face turned upward toward the Gul mohar branches.

"Four days away, and I missed this tree," she said softly.

I glanced at her, the way the lamplight threaded through her hair.

I thought: *This is the moment. Say it now.*

But I didn't. Not yet.

As we parted that night at the fork in the road, Mira waved lightly. "Good night, Aditya."

"Good night," I said.

But as I watched her walk away, I felt something stir inside me. The four empty days had been unbearable; her return had shown me how much of myself was now tied to her presence.

I couldn't let hesitation write the ending again.

The next chance, I promised myself, I wouldn't waste.

Back in my room that night, I sat by the window, the city lights blinking faintly against the horizon. Mira's laughter from our walk still echoed in my ears. But alongside it was the silence of the three days she'd been gone, a silence that had almost hollowed me out.

The contrast was unbearable. How could four days without her feel like an absence carved into my very bones? And how could a single evening with her restore so much light?

The answer was obvious, yet I had refused to say it aloud.

I loved her.

And love, left unsaid, was nothing but another name for regret.

I opened the drawer where the ring lay, still in its box. The infinity symbol gleamed faintly in the dim light, a quiet reminder of everything I hadn't done.

I picked it up, turning it over in my hand. The weight felt heavier than silver. It was the weight of all my hesitation, my excuses, my fear of losing what I hadn't even claimed.

I pressed the box shut and whispered, "Not again. Not this time."

The next morning, as I dressed for work, I caught my reflection in the mirror.

I looked tired not from work, but from carrying unspoken feelings. The lines of restraint, the shadows of unsaid words, were etched into my face more than sleeplessness ever could.

And I thought: *If I keep choosing silence, this is who I'll become forever. A man who walks beside love but never reaches out to touch it.*

The thought jolted me. It wasn't just about Mira anymore. It was about who I was becoming.

That evening, as I walked toward the Gul mohar tree, I imagined two futures unfolding.

In one, Mira left for Mumbai without ever knowing how I felt. She might remember me as a quiet friend, a walking companion, someone safe but distant. And I would remain here, haunted by what I never said, carrying the ring in a drawer like a relic of my own failure.

In the other, I told her. I risked everything awkwardness, rejection, even the possibility of losing the fragile closeness we had. But at least, in that future, I would know. At least I would not wonder forever.

For the first time, the second future felt less frightening than the first.

That night, standing beneath the Gul mohar, watching its branches sway gently against the evening sky, I made the decision.

The next chance I had whether over coffee, during a walk, or in the unlikeliest of moments, I would tell her.

Not with rehearsed lines, not with grand gestures, but simply, honestly.

Because the cost of silence was no longer bearable.

As I returned home, the city settling into its nightly hum, I carried the promise with me like a quiet flame. This wasn't about waiting for the perfect time anymore. This was about refusing to let time slip past unclaimed.

Mira might still leave for Mumbai. She might not feel the same. The story might not unfold the way I hoped.

But at least, I would not be left with the ache of the unsaid. Lying in bed, the ring box on the table beside me, I whispered into the dark:

"Next time, I'll speak."

And for the first time in weeks, I fell asleep not with the weight of regret, but with the fragile lightness of resolve.

# Delhi
# Part - 2

# DELHI

---

*4 Years Later*

---

The city was Delhi now. Not Bangalore's leafy lanes and Gul mohar trees, but Delhi's wide, restless roads, its heavy air, and its metro humming beneath the surface like an endless circulatory system.

Four years had passed since those evenings of quiet walks and Gul mohar shadows. In that time, I had shed versions of myself the way snakes shed their skin sometimes reluctantly, sometimes necessarily.

I wasn't the same Aditya anymore.

The water had become my refuge. Each morning, I swam laps at the community pool near my apartment. The rhythm of it, stroke, breathe, glide, gave me a discipline I had once lacked. My body had changed too; leaner, stronger, more defined.

There was something cleansing about the water. Every dive felt like erasing yesterday's dust, every stroke like carving out space for today.

When I climbed out of the pool, droplets streaming down my face, I felt almost fresh.

I toweled off, pulled on a plain white t-shirt, and walked to the counter where the pool staff kept our phones. Mine was cold from the air-conditioning, the screen dark. I turned on the internet, and the notifications began to pour in. Among the clutter of emails and work messages, one stood out.

*Aditi: Where are you? Don't tell me you're lost again. I'm waiting.*

I felt my lips curve into a smile I hadn't realized was forming. My thumbs typed back quickly:

*I'll be there in an hour.*

The typing dots appeared almost immediately, followed by:

*Be quick. And this time, no excuses.*

I chuckled to myself, slipping the phone into my pocket.

An hour later, I walked toward the small restaurant tucked into one of Delhi's crowded neighborhoods. The evening sun was low, the city painted in dusty gold.

Just as I was about to enter, the door swung open, and a girl in a red kurta stepped out. She was laughing at something on her phone, her hair catching the light in a way that momentarily stilled me.

Red kurta. Jasmine fragrance in the air. A fleeting smile.

And suddenly, the years peeled away. Bangalore rose in front of me again - the Gul mohar tree, the metro rides, Mira's laughter echoing in narrow lanes.

It lasted only a second, but it was enough. A memory like a wave, pulling me under before letting me go.

I blinked, and the girl was gone, swallowed by Delhi's crowd. I stood still for a moment, my hand on the door, my heart unexpectedly heavy. It wasn't her. Of course it wasn't her. But memory is cruel, it doesn't ask permission. It just arrives, uninvited, carrying with it both sweetness and ache. I exhaled slowly, forcing myself back into the present. This was Delhi, not Bangalore. This was now, not then.

I pushed open the door and stepped inside. Aditi was there, seated at a corner table, her long hair falling in waves over her shoulders. She wore a soft peach top, earrings that caught the light when she turned toward me.

Her eyes narrowed as I approached. "Why can't you ever be on time?"

I raised my hands in apology, sliding into the chair opposite her. "Sorry for keeping you waiting. The pool stretched longer than I thought."

She rolled her eyes, but there was a softness behind the mock annoyance. "One day you'll realize punctuality is not optional, Aditya."

I smiled faintly, but inside, I was still shaking off the ghost of the red kurta.

Aditi's eyes had that sharp clarity that could make a person feel both seen and exposed. She looked at me across the table, arms folded, her half-smile betraying amusement more than irritation.

"Three months," she said, tapping her spoon on the table lightly. "Three months of knowing you, and you still make me wait. Do you treat everyone this way, or am I just lucky?"

Her tone was teasing, but there was an undercurrent of something real in it, a question waiting for more than a joke.

I chuckled, picking up the menu. "Maybe you're just patient enough to put up with me."

She raised a brow. "Don't flatter yourself. I'm patient, but only up to a point."

Her words hung in the air, not threatening, but heavy enough to remind me that she wasn't here just for idle companionship.

Aditi had entered my life unexpectedly. We had met through a mutual friend at a book launch. I remembered her that evening standing confidently near the mic, asking a sharp question to the author, her voice steady, her curiosity unafraid. Later, we had been introduced, and conversation had come easily, surprisingly so. In three months, she had carved a place in my routine. Coffee after work, walks in Delhi's uneven parks, long texts about her job, her dreams, her favorite films.

And then one evening, out of nowhere, she had said it plainly: *"Aditya, I like you. More than just as a friend."*

I hadn't known what to say.

I hadn't accepted, but I hadn't denied either.

Instead, I had told her: *"Let's give it time. Let's just be and see where it goes."*

It had been my compromise, honest enough not to mislead, cautious enough not to commit.

Aditi had agreed, but I often caught in her eyes a quiet impatience, a question she never quite asked again but always carried.

As the waiter brought us food, she leaned back and said, "You know, Aditya, most people either say yes or no. You're the only one I've met who invented a third option."

I smiled faintly. "I guess I'm not most people."

Her expression softened. "No, you're not."

She reached across the table then, almost casually, her fingers brushing mine before retreating. The touch was light, but it left a warmth behind.

I looked at her, really looked, and felt the tug of something undeniable. Aditi was present - attentive, warm, alive with her own kind of brightness. She deserved more than hesitation.

But inside me, there was still the echo of the girl in the red kurta, the Gul mohar tree, the unsaid words that had shaped me. Mira's absence had taught me what hesitation cost but also left me cautious in ways I couldn't easily undo.

So, I smiled, ate, listened. I gave her pieces of myself, but never the whole.

"Aditya," she said after a pause, "I'm not asking for answers tonight. But don't keep me waiting forever, okay?"

Her voice wasn't demanding, it was almost tender, as if she knew I was still fighting something invisible.

I nodded slowly. "I won't."

And I meant it. At least, I wanted to mean it.

As Aditi spoke about her day the chaos of her office, the client who couldn't decide what they wanted, I found myself drifting. Not because she was dull; Aditi was never dull. But because somewhere in the folds of her words, an old memory stirred.

A red kurta. A jasmine fragrance.

I forced myself back to the present, nodding, smiling at Aditi's animated hand gestures. But the past has a way of slipping through cracks, especially when left unresolved.

Four years hadn't erased Bangalore.

The evenings of walking beside Mira, the silence that felt companionable, the notebook she carried with its secret lists, all of it was etched into me. The city had changed, perhaps; the Gul mohar tree may or may not still bloom the same way. But in my mind, those streets remained alive, suspended in a kind of timelessness.

And sometimes, without warning, they pulled me back.

Aditi reached for her glass of water, and my hand brushed against the table, instinctively touching the place where, years ago, I had hidden a ring box in my pocket.

The infinity ring. Simple, silver, shaped like a promise I never voiced.

It still sat in a drawer, though not here in Delhi. I had carried it with me when I moved, unable to leave it behind. A relic, a reminder.

I wondered what Mira was doing now. Was she still in Mumbai? Did she walk under Gul mohar trees there? Did she tick items off her notebook list? Did she ever think of Bangalore, of me? Her mobile was not reachable after she left.

"You've gone quiet again," Aditi said, pulling me out of the spiral. Her eyes searched mine, curious but not accusing. "Where do you go when you do that?"

I hesitated, then smiled faintly. "Old memories. They sneak up sometimes."

She tilted her head. "Good ones or bad ones?"

I thought for a moment. "Both."

She didn't press further. Instead, she reached for a piece of bread and said lightly, "Well, as long as you come back from them."

Her patience humbled me. Mira had been the shadow I carried, but Aditi was light offered freely, without demands. She didn't ask me to be someone else; she only asked that I not vanish into the past entirely.

Still, I wondered was it fair to let her walk beside me when my heart still carried echoes of someone else?

To steer the silence, I asked her about her photography hobby. Her face lit up instantly.

"You remembered," she said, surprised.

"Of course."

She described how she loved capturing Delhi's contradictions, the chaos of Chandni Chowk, the symmetry of Lodhi Gardens, the quiet corners of Connaught Place at dusk.

As she spoke, I realized she was teaching me something without meaning to how to love the present city, the present moment, without comparing it endlessly to what was lost.

I sat back, listening, caught between two worlds, the Bangalore etched in memory, and the Delhi unfolding before me through Aditi's words.

Both were real. Both shaped me.

But only one stood in front of me now, asking not for promises, but simply for presence.

When we left the restaurant, Delhi's evening was alive with its usual contradictions: honking traffic mixed with the fragrance of roasting corn on street carts, neon signs blinking against the darkening sky.

Aditi walked beside me, her scarf brushing lightly in the breeze. She wasn't in a hurry, though she could have been, she always walked with a kind of deliberate ease, as though she knew the city would eventually move around her.

"So," she said, glancing at me, "do you always take this long to let people in?"

The question was half-playful, half-serious.

I smiled faintly. "I guess I do."

"And is it worth the wait?" she asked, her tone teasing but her eyes searching.

I met her gaze. "I hope so."

As we walked, I couldn't help but think of Bangalore evenings, the filter coffee, Mira's sudden laughter, the way silence between us had once been enough. But tonight was different. Aditi wasn't silence; she was insistence, presence, a reminder that life didn't wait for hesitation. Where Mira had taught me the beauty of unsaid companionship, Aditi was teaching me the courage of spoken truth, of showing up.

And maybe I needed both lessons.

At the end of the lane, Aditi stopped. "You know," she said, "I'm not asking you to decide everything right now. But I want you to know, I'm here. Not forever, not with endless patience. But here. For now."

Her honesty was striking, almost disarming. There was no drama in her words, no demand. Just clarity.

I nodded slowly. "That means more than you think."

She smiled softly. "Then don't make me wait too long to find out what I mean to you."

Later, back in my Delhi apartment, I sat by the window, the city lights scattering across the horizon. My swimming bag lay by the chair, damp towel half-folded, phone buzzing with another message from Aditi:

*Next time, no delays. Good night, Aditya.*

I typed back: *Good night, Aditi. And thank you.*

Her reply came instantly: *For what?*

I stared at the screen before typing: *For being patient.*

Three dots blinked, then vanished. She didn't reply, and I didn't need her to.

# Mutual Friend

It was Aditi's idea. "Aditya," she said one evening over coffee, "you've been in Delhi for almost a year now and you still haven't seen Qutub Minar. How can you live in this city and not see its heart?"

I smiled at her enthusiasm. She had this way of treating Delhi like a living museum, every corner a story, every ruin a whisper from history.

"You sound like a tour guide," I teased.

She swatted my arm lightly. "Come tomorrow. No excuses."

And so, the plan was made.

The next afternoon we stood at the entrance. Qutub Minar rose ahead, sharp and majestic, its red sandstone catching the late sun like fire trapped in stone. Around us, the ruins of ancient mosques and courtyards stretched wide, alive with tourists, families, schoolchildren, and the occasional guide speaking rapid rehearsed lines in half a dozen languages.

Aditi's eyes shone as she lifted her camera. "Look at that detail!" she exclaimed, zooming in on the delicate carvings spiraling up the minaret.

I nodded, letting her excitement wash over me.

Aditi quickly slipped into her element. She wandered from arch to arch, crouching low for angles, tilting her head, waiting for light to hit a surface just so. She was patient and meticulous, like the city itself was her subject, not just her hobby.

"Don't move!" she called at one point, snapping a candid photo of me sitting on a low stone ledge.

I groaned. "You know I hate pictures."

She grinned. "Which is exactly why I take them. You'll thank me someday."

Her laughter drifted across the courtyard as she darted away toward another ruined wall.

I stayed behind, sitting under the shade of a weathered tree. The air was cool, filled with the hum of voices and the occasional call of birds. Children ran past, their laughter bouncing off the stones.

But my eyes were fixed on the minaret. Its height, its persistence through centuries of storms and rulers, humbled me.

It struck me how much had changed in four years. Bangalore felt like a different lifetime, yet echoes of it sometimes rose unbidden, like the red kurta outside the restaurant last week.

I closed my eyes, letting the weight of history and memory blur together.

Aditi was somewhere behind the archways, clicking, framing, creating her own story. I didn't mind her absence, it gave me space to breathe, to let my thoughts wander without the need for conversation.

I thought of how Delhi had become my city now: the metro rides, the pools, the quiet evenings by myself. Aditi had brought color into it, yes, but I had built it on my own first.

I was just beginning to relax when a voice, familiar yet unexpected, pierced through the noise around me.

"Aditya?"

I turned toward the voice, blinking against the sun. There she was Ramya.

It took me a second to place her. The last time I'd seen her was in Bangalore, four years ago, at that dinner I had so carefully planned and so miserably failed. She hadn't changed much: the same sharp, curious eyes, the same easy smile. Only now, a camera hung around her neck, confirming her identity before her words did.

"Ramya," I said slowly, almost uncertainly.

Her eyes widened, and then her face broke into delight. "I knew it was you! What are you doing here, in Delhi?"

I stood up, still reeling from the unexpectedness of it all. "I live here now. Work brought me."

She shook her head in disbelief, laughing. "Unbelievable. Of all places, of all moments, I run into you at Qutub Minar? What are the odds?"

Her laughter was infectious, but inside, I felt a tug of unease. Because where Ramya was, the shadow of Mira was never far.

We exchanged a few pleasantries. She told me she had been traveling for photography projects, capturing heritage sites across India. Delhi was her stop for a couple of months.

"And you?" she asked, tilting her head. "Still in finance, I assume. You always had that… numbers kind of face."

I chuckled nervously. "Yes. Still in finance."

She grinned. "Figures."

But then, as naturally as one might comment on the weather, she asked:

"And Mira? How is she?"

Her words fell into the space between us like a stone into still water, sending ripples through everything I had built to keep the past quiet.

I stared at her, stunned. "Mira?"

"Yes," she said, surprised at my hesitation. "Your Mira. Don't tell me you lost touch? I thought you two would've been married by now."

The courtyard around me seemed to fade, the voices, the children, even the towering minaret. Only her words remained.

I swallowed hard. "Ramya… I… I don't know. I haven't spoken to her in years."

Ramya's brows furrowed. "What? But" she stopped, clearly puzzled. "She changed her number, yes, but I thought surely, you'd still be in touch. She told me…"

Her voice trailed off, leaving me hanging in silence.

Inside me, something heavy shifted. Mira. Marriage. Words I had never connected in reality, only in secret daydreams, were being spoken aloud by someone else as if they were the most natural expectation in the world.

Ramya's eyes narrowed as she studied my blank expression. "Wait," she said slowly. "Don't tell me you really didn't know."

"Didn't know what?" I asked, my throat dry.

She let out a breath, half disbelieving, half exasperated. "That Mira was in love with you."

The words struck me like a blow. For a moment, I wasn't sure I had heard her right.

"What?" I managed to whisper.

Ramya folded her arms, shaking her head. "Oh my god. She told me so many times, Aditya. About you. About those evening walks under the Gul mohar tree, your quiet talks, the way you never rushed her. She adored that about you. She said you made her feel… seen."

I was frozen. The world around us kept moving tourists laughing, cameras clicking, but for me, time had stopped.

Ramya leaned closer, lowering her voice. "Even that night in Bangalore the dinner where I joined you? She told me on the way, 'Please don't say anything to Aditya. Not yet. I'll tell him when it feels right.' She wanted me to keep quiet."

I felt my knees weaken. I remembered that night vividly, the ring hidden in my pocket, my silence, my disappointment when she brought Ramya along. I had thought she was indifferent, that I was alone in my feelings.

And all along, she had felt the same.

"I…" My voice broke. "I never knew. She never said a word."

Ramya's expression softened. "That was Mira. She believed love had to come out naturally, without forcing it. She thought you'd say it first, and that when you did, it would mean everything."

My hands trembled slightly as I pressed them against my knees. All the nights of hesitation, the excuses, the silent walks, they crashed over me now like waves of regret.

"She loved me?" I whispered again, as if repeating it might help me believe it.

Ramya nodded firmly. "Yes. Without a doubt."

Ramya placed a hand lightly on my arm. "Aditya, Mira changed her number. She cut herself off for reasons I still don't know. But before she left, she told me one thing clearly: she loved you. And she believed you loved her. She thought you'd eventually find a way to tell her."

Her eyes softened. "She was waiting for you."

The words carved through me, sharper than stone. Mira had waited. And I had stayed silent

I hadn't noticed Aditi approaching from behind the archway, her camera hanging loosely at her side. She must have returned from her wandering just in time to hear fragments "Mira," "love," "evening walks," "waiting for him to say it."

When I glanced up, she was standing a few feet away, her brows knitted in confusion, her lips parted as though caught between stepping forward and stepping back.

Ramya followed my gaze and turned. "Oh—hello. I didn't mean to intrude on your time. I was just catching up with an old… friend."

But the look on Aditi's face told me she had heard enough to know this was not just casual catching up.

In that moment, I felt as though I were standing at a crossroads between two lives:

- The life I had almost lived with Mira, had she and I both found the courage to speak.
- And the life I was now cautiously, tentatively, building with Aditi.

The past and present had collided, and both were staring me in the face.

And I, as always, was silent.

Aditi finally walked closer, her camera swaying against her hip. Her voice was calm, but her eyes betrayed a storm. "Aditya," she said softly, "who is Mira?"

The question was simple, but it carried the weight of an entire past I had never spoken about.

I opened my mouth, then closed it again. Words, always my weakness, betrayed me now.

Aditi didn't speak at first. She just stood there, the Qutub Minar towering behind her like a reminder of centuries that outlasted human confusion. Finally, she said, "So all this time, you've been… carrying her."

Her voice wasn't angry, it was weary, as if she had suddenly been asked to share a burden she never knew existed.

I took a step toward her. "Aditi, I'm not with her. I haven't seen her in years. But yes… she's still a part of me. I can't pretend otherwise."

Her eyes glistened, though she blinked quickly. "And what part of you is left for me, Aditya?"

For a moment, the three of us stood in silence:

- Me, crushed under the weight of what I never said.
- Ramya, the accidental messenger of truths too long hidden.

- Aditi, caught in the crossfire between a past she had never asked for and a present she had begun to hope for.

Around us, tourists snapped pictures, children laughed, guides recited history. But for us, time had narrowed to this unbearable moment.

As Aditi turned slightly away, her face unreadable, I realized something painful: silence had once cost me Mira. And if I wasn't careful, it might cost me Aditi too.

For the first time, I saw clearly how hesitation doesn't just belong to the past it follows you, infects the present, and threatens the future.

And under the looming shadow of Qutub Minar, I knew: a choice had to be made.

# The Calling bell

---

*4 Years Back*

---

The sound of the calling bell was sharp but not jarring it was familiar, like the pulse of expectation itself. I rushed to the door, my breath caught somewhere between nervousness and hope. And there she was.

Mira.

Her hair, loosened from the day's humidity, fell softly over her shoulders. The faint fragrance of jasmine clung to her, as though she carried with her the very essence of our evening walks. She smiled, not hurriedly, not shyly, just enough to make my heart stumble into chaos.

"You're early," I said, though I had no idea what time it was. In dreams, time folds on itself.

She stepped inside, and suddenly my flat seemed brighter, more alive.

I excused myself for a second, nerves prickling. The ring box, yes, the ring box I had stared at the night before was still on the table beside my bed. I had taken it out, held it, turned it over in my hands, whispering questions to myself that had no answers.

Now, as I tried to tuck it back into the cupboard, my hand slipped.

The box tumbled to the floor with a dull, soft thud.

Mira's voice floated in from the living room. "Aditya? Everything alright?"

And before I could grab it, she was there, standing in the doorway. Her eyes dropped to the box on the floor, then rose to meet mine.

For one fragile second, silence filled the room. The kind of silence that demands courage.

"This…" My voice cracked. I bent, picked up the box, and held it out awkwardly, almost defensively. But then something inside me shifted, the years of hesitation, the endless unsaid words. They cracked open.

"This is for you, Mira."

I opened it, and the ring gleamed like it had been waiting for this moment too. My chest felt tight, my throat dry, but the words came.

"Will you marry me?"

Her lips parted in surprise, her eyes shimmering with sudden tears. Then she smile, a smile that was relief, joy, and love all at once.

"Yes," she whispered, stepping closer. "Yes, I do."

The words hung in the air, golden, sacred.

We moved into each other's arms, and the world blurred. The scent of her hair, the warmth of her skin, the way her heartbeat pressed against mine, it was real, achingly real.

I held her, tighter than I ever had in walking life. All the evenings of walking side by side, all the silences we had protected, all the words left unsaid, they collapsed into this single embrace, sealing everything.

For once, there was no hesitation. No fear. No distance.

It was just us.

And in that embrace, I felt the life we could have lived: morning coffees, shared books, quiet fights, reconciliations, laughter echoing through rooms.

The infinity symbol on the ring wasn't just metal. It was a promise.

But then like a crack splitting the sky, the calling bell rang again.

Louder. Sharper. Relentless.

Mira's form blurred, her warmth slipping away from my arms. I tried to hold on, but she was fading, like mist in the sun.

"No," I whispered. "Don't go."

The bell kept ringing. It was a dream!

And I opened my eyes.

The sharp buzz of the calling bell jolted me fully awake. My arms, still half-extended as though holding onto someone, clutched at emptiness. The warmth, the scent, the "Yes, I do" all of it had vanished like smoke.

I sat up, breathing hard. The room was pale with early morning light. 7 a.m., the clock on the wall told me. Too early for dreams to feel this real. Too late to go back and finish them.

The bell rang again. Urgent. Insistent.

For one dizzy, reckless heartbeat, I thought *It's her. Mira. It has to be.*

I stumbled out of bed, rubbing sleep from my eyes. My heart raced, tripping over itself in its eagerness.

I caught my reflection in the mirror by the bathroom door: hair sticking up wildly, sleep still clinging to my face. I splashed cold water, ran my hands through my hair, gargled quickly as though preparing for an exam I hadn't studied for.

*She can't see me like this,* I thought absurdly. *Not when I'm about to*

I froze. About to what? Propose? Confess? Continue the dream where it left off?

The bell rang a third time.

I padded barefoot across the room, every step heavier with expectation. My hand hovered above the latch, trembling slightly.

What if it really was Mira? What if fate, for once, had decided to give me another chance, right here, right now?

In my head, I rehearsed hurried words: *"Mira, I...."* No. Too rushed.

Maybe: *"There's something I've been meaning to tell you..."*

Or perhaps no words at all, just the box, just the gesture, just the truth unshackled.

My throat went dry.

Behind that door could be everything I had wanted and feared. The dream was still sticky in my chest, its echoes confusing my sense of reality. I could almost see her waiting there, tilting her head, jasmine scent announcing her before her smile.

I closed my eyes for a second, inhaled deeply, and whispered to myself: *Don't hesitate this time. Don't.*

The bell rang once more, impatiently.

I gripped the handle, my heart thudding against my ribs.

And then, I pulled the door open.

The door swung open, and for a heartbeat my breath stopped. But it wasn't Mira.

It was my cousin brother, Rohit, standing there with two bulging backpacks, a grin spread across his face as if the world belonged to him. His hair was slightly messy from travel, his T-shirt clung to him with the dust of an early journey, and his eyes sparkled with their usual mischief.

"Surprise!" he announced, throwing up his arms like he'd just pulled off a magic trick.

I blinked. My body, still tense with expectation, struggled to recalibrate. The dream's echo still rang in me the "Yes, I do," the warmth of Mira's embrace. To see Rohit here, so solidly real, was like crashing back into gravity after floating.

"You?" I managed, my voice uneven.

"Yes, me!" Rohit laughed, brushing past me into the apartment as though he owned the place. "Who else did you expect this early in the morning? The milkman?"

His words landed with a cruel irony. I swallowed hard, masking the collapse inside me with a forced smile.

He dropped his bags onto the floor with a heavy thud. "Man, that was a long bus ride. I should get a medal for surviving Bengaluru traffic even before sunrise. And you look half-dead. Were you sleeping or daydreaming?"

"Something like that," I murmured, closing the door slowly.

He was already moving around the room, peering at my plants, fiddling with my books, opening the fridge as if to confirm my bachelor habits. His presence was a whirlwind, filling every corner of my quiet space.

I leaned against the wall, watching him. Inside me, disappointment curled like a fist. I had wanted it be Mira at the door. For once, I had been ready.

But here was Rohit, grinning, alive, carrying the noise of family and the weight of the ordinary.

So, I smiled, hid the ache, and said, "You could've at least called."

He winked. "Where's the fun in that? A surprise is only a surprise if it's inconvenient."

As he chattered about his plans, how long he might stay, the people he wanted to meet in the city, I nodded absently. But my mind kept slipping back to the dream, the ring, Mira's voice.

It felt so close, so real, and yet here I was, making tea for my cousin, pretending nothing had happened.

The infinity I had almost reached dissolved into the clatter of cups and the sound of Rohit humming tunelessly by the window.

And once again, the unsaid lodged itself in my chest.

The kettle whistled faintly as I poured hot water over the tea leaves, steam clouding the kitchen window. Rohit was still talking, his voice bouncing from one story to another bus ride, a fight he overheard between two passengers, the funny slogans painted on trucks.

I smiled in the right places, nodded when necessary, but inside I was still standing in my bedroom, still holding Mira's hand, still hearing her say *"Yes, I do."*

The scent of tea was grounding, but also cruel. I wanted jasmine, not cardamom. Dreams have a strange cruelty. They give you everything in the softest, most tender way, only to snatch it away the second you open your eyes. And sometimes, like now, they give you more clarity than waking life ever does.

In the dream, I had not hesitated. I had spoken. And she had said yes.

If only I could fold the dream into reality. But the calling bell had ripped me out of that world and into this one: Rohit's bags by the door, his laughter filling the air, the mundane weight of family obligations. I watched him as he sipped his tea noisily, leaning back against the sofa. He was comfort in his own way, family, familiarity, the reminder that life was more than love and longing. But he was also a curtain, blocking me from the world I wanted to step into, the world where Mira had been standing with tears in her eyes and a yes on her lips.

The contrast was almost unbearable.

That morning, I realized something I had been avoiding I loved her. Mira. Deeply. Irrevocably.

Not as a maybe. Not as a silence. Not as a someday.

The dream had stripped me bare and shown me what I wanted, what I feared, and what I kept postponing. But when the door opened, it wasn't Mira. It was life, in the form of my cousin brother, barging in with backpacks and stories, reminding me that not everything waits for love to find its courage.

Rohit stretched his legs, yawned, and said cheerfully, “Feels good to be here, Yaar. I’ll crash for a bit, then let’s explore the city later.”

I nodded, forcing a smile, hiding the storm behind my ribs.

The dream’s aftertaste lingered as I looked at the door, still half expecting it to ring again, still half hoping she’d be there.

But there was only Rohit, standing in my flat, so alive, so ordinary while Mira remained a ghost I carried, a yes, I had never heard in waking life.

# Fate of Unsaid

---

*4 Years Later - Present*

---

The Qutub Minar loomed behind us, its shadow stretching across the courtyard like time itself pressing down on my chest. Tourists laughed, cameras clicked, children darted between ancient stones, but for me, all sound had dulled.

Aditi stood a few feet away, her camera strap clutched tight in her hand. Her face was unreadable, half confusion, half quiet demand.

Her eyes locked on mine. "Aditya," she said slowly, each word steady, "were you in love with her?" Mira.

The name wasn't spoken, but it hung between us like a ghost, more real than the monument towering behind.

My throat constricted. I opened my mouth, but nothing came out. What was I supposed to say?

Yes? That I had loved Mira with everything I had but had never dared to speak it?

No? That would be a lie, a betrayal to myself.

The silence stretched. Aditi's eyes flickered, searching me for something truth, denial, anything at all.

But I just stood there, trapped in the old prison of hesitation.

She let out a shaky breath, her voice softer now. “I need to understand, Aditya. Because from where I stand, it feels like she loved you, and you… you just didn’t know.”

Her tone wasn’t accusing it was worse. It was pained.

I lowered my gaze, shame prickling at the back of my neck. “Aditi, I…” The words dissolved. The truth felt too heavy to lift.

Ramya, sensing the intimacy of the moment, took a small step away. Her eyes darted between us, guilt softening her face. She hadn’t intended to light this fire, but the flames now danced freely, unstoppable.

“I’ll give you two a moment,” she murmured, before slipping into the background of the ruins.

But Aditi’s eyes never left me.

For a long minute, neither of us spoke. The air was thick with things unsaid, my past with Mira, Aditi’s present feelings, the shadow of what could have been and the question of what could be.

Finally, Aditi whispered, “You can’t even say it, can you?”

Her words weren’t angry. They were simply… tired.

And in that exhaustion, I saw the weight my silence placed not just on me, but on her too.

Aditi took a step forward. Her camera dangled loosely at her side now, forgotten. The tourists, the sun, the monument all faded into background noise.

Her voice was steady, though her eyes glistened. “You know what hurts, Aditya? Not that you loved someone before me. Not even that you couldn’t tell her. What hurts is this right now, you can’t even look me in the eye and tell me what you feel.”

I swallowed hard, every muscle in me taut.

She stopped just a breath away from me. "I don't want to be another Mira in your story. A shadow. A silence. Someone you carry inside but never speak to."

Her words pierced deeper than any accusation.

Then she inhaled, steadying herself, and said it plainly:

"I'm in love with you, Aditya."

The air seemed to still. My pulse hammered in my ears. Her confession was everything Mira's hadn't been clear, brave, undeniable. She wasn't leaving space for ambiguity. She wasn't waiting for time or fate.

She was telling me now, in the present, with no fear of rejection. And me? I stood there, tongue-tied, heart aching with the weight of all the words I had never learned to say.

"I needed you to know," Aditi whispered, her voice breaking slightly. "Even if you can't say it back. Even if you never will. At least this way, I won't leave wondering if you ever knew. I won't walk away as another secret that died in your silence."

She brushed at her cheek quickly, almost angrily. "I deserve more than that, Aditya. Don't you think?"

Her courage shone in the way she stood there fragile but unflinching.

I wanted to answer. I wanted to reach for her hand, to give her the certainty she had earned.

But Mira's name echoed in me, Mira's laughter, Mira's absence. The ghost had tightened its grip. So, I said nothing. My lips parted, closed, parted again. Only silence spilled out. And in that silence, I watched Aditi's eyes dim, though she nodded faintly, as if she had expected it.

I couldn't stay there any longer between Aditi's brave confession and my own choking silence. Ramya had slipped away, wisely giving us space, but even the empty courtyard pressed on me.

So, I mumbled something about needing air, about needing time, and I walked. Aditi didn't stop me. Her stillness behind me was louder than any protest.

***

An hour later, I was at the swimming pool. The blue water rippled gently, inviting, but I didn't enter. I had changed into my swimwear automatically, more out of habit than intention, and now sat at the edge of the pool, legs dangling, toes brushing the surface.

The air smelled of chlorine, sharp and clean. Around me, laughter from children learning to float mixed with the steady instructions of a coach. But even their noise felt far away.

I stared into the water, seeing not my reflection but Mira's smile, Mira's silence, Mira's absence.

Why hadn't I told her? The question gnawed at me, the same way it had for four years.

Fear, yes. But fear of what? Of rejection? Of ruining the fragile comfort of our walks? Of exposing myself, only to find her feelings didn't mirror mine?

Or was it something deeper; an instinct to protect silence, to keep love safe by never testing it in the light of words? Perhaps I thought time would give me courage. Perhaps I believed the right moment would arrive on its own. But time had passed. Moments had gone. And she had slipped away.

Maybe that was why she was unreachable now. Why Ramya had no number, no address, no way to find her. Maybe the universe had closed that door because I had never opened it when I could. And yet, even here, now, Aditi had stood in front of me, clear and vulnerable, and I had frozen. Had I learned nothing? Or was hesitation so woven into me that I couldn't cut it loose?

The water lapped gently against my feet, cool and unbothered. I clenched my fists. Aditi deserved better than silence. Mira had deserved better too.

And maybe this was my curse: to carry both the love I had never confessed and the love I might lose the same way.

I sat there for a long time, the pool's surface reflecting the city lights as evening descended, wondering if courage was something that could be found at all, or if it had to be chosen.

By the time the pool emptied, and the children had left with their parents, I was still sitting there, unmoved. The lifeguard gave me a strange look before switching off half the lights, leaving the water in dusky blue shadows.

I still hadn't swum a single lap. My body was ready, but my mind was anchored somewhere else.

Silence had cost me once. It was about to cost me again.

The ache was unbearable.

I closed my eyes. And in the darkness behind my lids, I saw her again. Mira, walking beside me in Bangalore, her laughter rising like sudden rain. Mira under the Gul mohar tree, her notebook pressed to her chest. Mira at the restaurant, introducing Ramya, hiding her secret behind her smile.

Ramya's words echoed: *She was in love with you. She was waiting for you.* I gritted my teeth. "Why didn't I see it?" The whisper left my mouth, barely audible, but heavy with regret. Maybe I had been blind. Maybe I had been a coward. Either way, I had lost her.

And yet had I?

Ramya didn't know where Mira was. She had disappeared into Mumbai, into her own life. But that didn't mean she was unreachable.

Was I willing to let her remain a ghost forever? Or did I owe it to both of us to at least try?

The fear rose quickly: what if I found her and she had moved on? Married? Forgotten me? Would it break me all over again?

But another thought was sharper: what if she hadn't? What if she was still waiting, in her own way, and I never even looked? I stood abruptly, the cool air clinging to my damp skin. Enough. Enough silence. Enough hesitation.

If I was cursed, it was by my own inaction. And the only way to end it was to move. To speak. To search.

For Mira. For the truth. For closure, if not for love.

I didn't know what I would find, or what it would cost. But I knew one thing clearly: I couldn't continue carrying her ghost without knowing if she was still alive in my story.

By the time I walked back to my apartment, my legs felt heavy but my mind sharper than it had in years.

I sat at my desk, switched on my laptop, and stared at the blank search bar. My fingers hovered, hesitant even now.

But then I typed her name. *Mira.*

The journey had to begin somewhere.

And as the screen blinked with results, I whispered to myself the promise I had once failed to keep:

"No more unsaid."

# Misconception

---

*4 Years Back*

---

The apartment felt strangely full of Rohit in it. It wasn't that he was noisy though he was but that his presence carried the dense, unfiltered energy of youth. The kind that left no space for silence to breathe.

Since he had arrived, my quiet world had been rearranged. My evenings were now filled with his chatter about college life, upcoming exams, new friendships, memes, and half-serious plans about starting a YouTube channel.

Everywhere he went, he left traces his earphones tangled on the sofa, his jacket on a chair, half-eaten packets of chips near the TV.

And yet, despite the chaos, I didn't mind. Rohit reminded me of a time when I used to laugh easily. When days felt long and uncomplicated.

It was a Thursday evening, a soft drizzle outside the kind Bangalore was known for. I had just returned from work, half-soaked, when Rohit greeted me from the couch.

"Bro, your city is awesome," he said, munching on something. "I walked to the bakery down the lane. Even the air smells like coffee."

I smiled faintly, hanging my jacket. "That's Bangalore for you."

He stretched. "By the way, someone's been asking about you."

I turned, confused. "Who?"

Before he could answer, the **calling bell** rang again.

I walked to the door, expecting maybe the milk delivery boy or the neighbor's kid. But when I opened it there, she was.

Mira.

She stood there, rain droplets glistening on her hair, her scarf slightly damp, her smile hesitant yet warm.

"Hey," she said softly.

"Hey," I echoed, my heartbeat doing a familiar, uncontrollable dance. "Come in."

She stepped inside, and her eyes widened when she noticed Rohit sitting on the couch.

"Oh," she said, caught off guard. "I didn't know you had company."

Rohit jumped up instantly, ever the extrovert. "Hi! I'm Rohit Aditya's cousin." Mira smiled politely. "Nice to meet you. I'm Mira." Something about the way she said her name gentle, unassuming made Rohit grin. "Ah, the famous Mira. I've heard your name a few times."

I shot him a warning look, but he ignored it, as usual. Mira laughed lightly, brushing a strand of wet hair behind her ear. "Famous, huh? I didn't know I was."

I went to the kitchen to make coffee, partly to escape the awkwardness. From there, I could hear them talking, their voices easy and casual. Rohit had that effect on people he made conversation seem effortless.

When I returned with three mugs, they were laughing about something probably one of Rohit's exaggerated college stories. The sight was oddly comforting. Mira fit into the space naturally, as though she had always belonged here.

For a fleeting second, I imagined a future where this wasn't rare, where she visited not as a guest, but as someone who lived here.

As we sipped coffee, Mira asked Rohit about his studies, his hometown, his plans. He answered everything with the open confidence of youth.

Then he turned the tables. "So, Mira, what about you? What do you do?"

She smiled. "I write. I'm working on some stories, and I also work for a small publishing firm nearby."

Rohit nodded approvingly. "A writer, huh? That's cool."

She laughed softly. "Depends on what day you ask. Some days, words listen. Most days, they don't."

Her voice had that quiet music that made even simple words sound like poetry.

Just then, my phone buzzed. It was from work something about a last-minute report. I excused myself reluctantly, slipping into my room.

As I took the call, I heard their voices continue faintly through the half-closed door. The rain outside tapped against the window, steady and rhythmic.

I had no idea that while I was busy talking about spreadsheets and deadlines, conversations in the living room were stitching misunderstandings that would change everything.

The faint sound of Aditya's voice drifted from his bedroom—muffled, serious, laced with the familiar tone of work. The moment his door clicked shut, Rohit leaned forward on the couch, eager to fill the space.

"So," he said, resting his mug on the table, "you and my cousin seem close. I mean, you visit often?"

Mira smiled politely. "Yes, we walk together sometimes in the evenings. Just... talk."

"Ah," Rohit said, his grin widening. "The famous evening walks. He told me about those."

Her eyes softened. "He did?"

"Of course. Though he conveniently left out that you're so much prettier in person," he teased.

Mira laughed, shaking her head. "You must be a handful at home."

"You have no idea."

There was a brief lull in conversation, comfortable but expectant. Then Rohit, always the one to fill silence, said lightly, "You know, I was just telling Aditya earlier he'll probably get married soon. Some alliance discussions are going on. My aunt's been hunting for matches."

Mira's smile faltered. "Married?"

"Yeah," Rohit said cheerfully, oblivious to the shift in her tone. "You know how families are. They've found a few potential matches, and he seems too lazy to object. I told him he should be honest with the girl he's seeing, but well… he's private like that."

Mira tried to keep her expression neutral, but something inside her clenched. She looked toward the closed bedroom door, hearing Aditya's distant voice, and suddenly the room felt smaller.

"Oh," she said softly. "I didn't know."

Rohit, still in his own world, continued. "Yeah, he doesn't talk about it much. But I can tell something's up. He's been thoughtful lately, like he's hiding something good. Maybe he's already found his person, who knows?"

He winked playfully, mistaking her silence for amusement.

Mira forced a faint smile, nodding. "Maybe he has."

Inside, her chest tightened.

To break the sudden heaviness in the air, Rohit leaned back and asked, "So what about you? What do you do when you're not torturing my cousin with long walks?"

Mira chuckled softly. "I write… and work with a small publishing company. But soon I might not be here."

"Oh?" Rohit asked.

"I'm moving to Mumbai in a few months," she said, trying to sound casual. "I got a good offer from a renowned company there"

He raised his brows. "Wow. Big move." She nodded, then added quietly, "And there's someone my parents want me to meet there."

Rohit sat up straighter, his grin returning. "Oh, so you're getting married too! Wow, perfect timing. Both of you will be busy with weddings this year!"

Mira blinked, momentarily thrown off, then gave a small, distant smile. "Yeah… maybe."

Rohit laughed, clinking his mug softly against hers like a toast. "See? Life sorts itself out. You two are too serious, you know. Everything works out in the end."

She smiled weakly, her throat tight.

And somewhere between his careless cheer and her unspoken heartache, the truth was buried.

The sound of the bedroom door opening broke the moment. Aditya stepped out, phone in hand, his face carrying that familiar post-call exhaustion.

"Sorry," he said, "work emergency." "And later mom called me! And asking about Marriage!"

Mira smiled, but her eyes didn't quite meet his. "It's okay."

He didn't notice. He never did.

They all chatted a bit lighter, surface-level things about food and movies. Mira excused herself soon after, saying she had an early morning.

As she stood at the door, Rohit said brightly, "Good luck with Mumbai! And with, you know…"

She smiled faintly. "Thanks."

Aditya frowned slightly. “Mumbai?”

But she was already turning toward the stairs, her voice soft as she said, “We’ll talk later. Good night, Aditya.”

And before he could ask, she was gone.

The apartment felt strangely empty once Mira closed the door behind her. The faint scent of her jasmine perfume still lingered in the air, mingling with the smell of freshly brewed coffee. Rohit stretched, yawning. “She’s nice,” he said casually. “You didn’t tell me she was so down-to-earth.”

I smiled, distracted, still half turned toward the door. “Yeah,” I murmured. “She’s… different.”

He smirked. “Different, huh? That’s code for something.”

I shot him a tired look. “Don’t start.”

He laughed, hands behind his head. “Relax, man. I’m not teasing. I really like her, she’s mature, funny, and she listens. That’s rare.”

I nodded absently, my mind elsewhere. Something about the way Mira had left so abruptly her eyes distant sat uneasily in me. I wanted to call her, to ask if everything was alright. But then Rohit spoke again, and everything changed.

“Anyway, good luck to her.”

I frowned. “Good luck?”

“Yeah,” he said, reaching for his cup. “With her future husband. She’s getting married, right?”

The words hit like a physical blow.

“What?” I said sharply, turning toward him.

Rohit blinked, confused. “Didn’t she tell you? She said she’s moving to Mumbai soon. Some new job, and her parents have found someone there. You didn’t know?”

I stared at him, my pulse roaring in my ears. “No. She didn’t tell me that.”

"Oh," Rohit said, taken aback. "I thought you knew. She mentioned it casually. Maybe there's someone her parents want her to meet there."

I sank into the couch, the room tilting slightly around me. Mira. Getting married. The idea didn't fit. It felt impossible, like hearing a language I should understand but couldn't. "She's… getting married," I repeated slowly.

"Yeah," Rohit said, still oblivious to the storm he'd unleashed. "She's great though, man. Whoever she's marrying is lucky."

I didn't respond. The sentence hung in the air like smoke, heavy and unbreathable.

That night, sleep refused to come.

Rohit fell asleep easily, snoring faintly from the next room, while I lay awake, staring at the ceiling fan spinning in lazy circles. The shadows it cast seemed to move with their own rhythm reminding me of things unsaid, moments lost.

I replayed the evening over and over. Her eyes when she said goodnight. Her soft tone when she mentioned Mumbai. I hadn't paid attention.

Maybe she *had* wanted to tell me. Maybe I'd made it too easy for her not to. I turned on my side, clutching the edge of my pillow. What if I had told her sooner? What if I hadn't let fear keep me quiet?

Would she still be leaving?

Would she still be marrying someone else?

The what ifs piled up, thick and relentless, until dawn slipped quietly into the window, and I was left with nothing but a hollow ache where hope used to live.

The next morning arrived slow and gray. Bangalore's light drizzle had settled into a quiet mist, the kind that seemed to blur the edges of everything.

Rohit was already awake, humming tunelessly as he packed his bag for college work. “Hey, bro,” he called from the other room. “You, okay? You look like you didn’t sleep.”

I forced a small smile. “Couldn’t.”

He nodded, zipping his bag. “Same here. This city’s too peaceful for me no traffic noises, no fights with auto drivers, no chaos. Feels weird.”

I didn’t respond. My head was still heavy from the night before, every thought circling back to Mira’s smile, her goodbye, and Rohit’s words: *‘She’s getting married.’*

Three days later, Rohit left.

He was cheerful as ever, waving from the cab, calling out, “Next time, I expect you to take me around! And maybe invite Mira too by then you both will be happily settled, who knows?”

I managed a weak smile, waving back as the taxi turned the corner.

The moment he disappeared; the apartment fell silent again, too silent. The way it used to be before his arrival. Except now, silence didn’t feel peaceful. It felt heavy.

That evening, I finally stepped out for a walk.

The familiar path, the one Mira and I always took looked the same, yet completely different. The trees were still shedding Gul mohar petals like quiet embers, the sky still blushing toward twilight. But there was no laughter beside me, no quiet companionship matching my steps.

I walked slower than usual, hoping to see her turn the corner, carrying her notebook, her scarf fluttering in the breeze.

But she didn’t come.

When I returned home, I sat on the edge of my bed, phone in hand. The screen’s glow painted the room in cold light.

My fingers hovered for a long time before I finally typed:

**“Let’s walk?”**

Just two words. Simple. Familiar. The ones that had started every evening with her.

I hit *send.*

Then I waited.

Minutes passed. The blue ticks never appeared.

I checked my phone again before sleeping. Nothing.

The next morning, nothing.

# Dinner

Morning, I sat with my cup of coffee and stared at the bougainvillea across the street. Their colors had deepened since the last rain a shade somewhere between magenta and memory. They reminded me of her, of course. Almost everything did now.

It had been days since I'd seen Mira. I tried to tell myself it was fine, that she must be busy. That maybe, like all things that begin without a reason, this too would fade without closure. But every time I passed the lane where we used to walk, something inside me tugged. That faint smell of jasmine from her body perfume, the sound of her footsteps beside mine, I remembered them too vividly to pretend I didn't care.

One evening, unable to take the quiet any longer, I went to the terrace. From up there, the city looked like a network of blinking lights each window a story, each streetlight a confession. The wind was cool, brushing against the small potted plants I'd kept by the railing. I watered them slowly, one by one, as if nurturing some forgotten part of myself.

And then I heard it.

A voice. Soft, uncertain, but familiar. "Aditya?"

The watering can tilted in my hand, spilling water on my shoe. I turned.

She was standing near the gate, Mira. Her presence felt both sudden and inevitable, like rain you can smell before it begins to fall.

She wore a pale blue kurta, simple and unassuming, her dupatta fluttering in the light breeze. Her hair was tied loosely, and the faintest trace of kajal lingered around her eyes, the same eyes that had once met mine across a crowded metro and somehow never left me.

I walked down to meet her, my heart doing the strange, uneven rhythm it reserved only for her.

"Mira," I said, trying to sound casual but failing miserably.

"You still keep your plants alive," she said, smiling gently.

"They're easier to talk to than people," I replied. That made her laugh the kind of short, soft laugh that always made the world feel lighter.

Then silence. The kind that holds words hostage.

Finally, I asked, "Why didn't you reply to my message?"

She looked down at her hands. "I was… caught up." "I've been planning to move," she said. "Things got a little hectic."

"You don't sound happy," she said, half-smiling, half-questioning. "I am," I lied. "Just… not good at goodbyes."

After a pause, I said, "I've applied for a transfer too." Her eyebrows lifted. "You?"
"Yeah," I said, forcing a small laugh. "To Delhi. Figured a change might do me good."

Her expression softened a mix of surprise and something unspoken. "Delhi," she repeated slowly. "Yeah. I guess I didn't want to stay here… without the familiar chaos."
She smiled faintly. "Without me, you mean?"

I hesitated. "Maybe."

That one word soft, ambiguous carried everything I didn't know how to say.

We talked about mundane things after that. About weather, the metro crowds, the new café opening. But underneath every casual sentence, I could feel the pulse of everything we weren't saying.

When she said she had to leave, I walked her to the gate. The sky had turned a deep violet, clouds gathering like secrets over the city. "Before you go," I said, "maybe we should… have dinner. You know, before both of us leave the city." She looked surprised for a moment, then smiled. "A parting dinner?" "If you'd like to call it that." She nodded. "Okay. One last dinner."

I watched her walk away, the echo of her steps fading with the evening traffic. I didn't move for a long time.

Later that night, I sat by my desk, staring at the small ring box I'd kept hidden behind some papers. I opened it, just for a second. The faint light from the lamp caught the silver glint of the infinity symbol on the ring, a quiet reminder of everything that could have been.

I closed the box again.

***

**Aditya**

The next few days moved like a slow song on repeat one you can't stop listening to even though it hurts. I tried to keep myself occupied with work, filling spreadsheets, attending calls, pretending numbers could somehow drown emotions. But she lingered everywhere.

Every evening, I looked out of the window hoping to see her walk by. Sometimes, I thought I caught a glimpse of her scarf fluttering past the gate, but it was never her. Just another stranger moving through a city that didn't care who stayed or who left.

One morning, as I scrolled absently through my emails, a new message blinked on my screen. It was from Mira. Just two words *"Dinner Friday?"* My fingers hovered over the keyboard longer than necessary before I typed back, *"Yes. 7:30?"* Her reply came instantly *"Done."*

That was all. But those four words filled my entire week.

I went through the motions of each day with an odd mix of anticipation and dread. I kept wondering if she'd mention her move again, or if she'd changed her mind. I wondered if she'd noticed how I'd hesitated the other day when she'd asked if I was going to miss her.

When Friday finally arrived, I left office early. I wanted time, time to think, time to choose the right words, time to prepare for a conversation I wasn't sure I'd have the courage to finish.

I reached the restaurant a few minutes early. It was a quiet place, tucked between two old buildings, with soft yellow lights and a faint scent of cardamom tea in the air. We'd been here once before, on a random evening after work when she'd insisted on trying their famous dish. That night, I'd watched her laugh so hard she'd cried when I dropped chutney on my shirt.

Now, I sat at the same table, straightening my shirt, checking my watch every few minutes.

I ordered two coffees before she arrived one black for me, one filter for her, a small act of memory that felt like love.

And then she walked in.

Time didn't stop, but it did something close. The whole place seemed to shift like air rearranging itself to make room for her. She wore the same red kurta - the same kurta in which I saw her the first time, her hair loose, small silver jhumkas swaying gently. There was something different about her maybe it was the faint sadness in her eyes, or the calm acceptance that comes just before goodbye.

"Hey," she said, sliding into the seat opposite mine. "Hey," I replied, unable to hide the smile that found me.

"You're early," she said. "I didn't want to risk Bangalore traffic stealing a moment from me," I said lightly.

She laughed, and for a few seconds, it felt like old times like everything between us had been paused instead of broken.

Her eyes sparkled for a moment. "You're really going, then?" "I am," I said quietly. "Got my transfer confirmed."

"That's fast," she said, smiling faintly. "I think they just wanted to get rid of me."

"Good for you," she said.

But the words sounded rehearsed, as though she had told herself to say them before walking in.

I hesitated, then asked, "And Mumbai?" "Still final," she said. "I leave in about four weeks."

Four weeks went fast! And remaining four weeks would ….

"I'll miss Bangalore," she said after a pause. "Or just the walks?" I asked.

Her eyes met mine, soft and distant. "Maybe both."

**Mira**

I had spent nearly half an hour staring at my own reflection before leaving to restaurant.
Not to admire myself, but to ask the mirror a question I couldn't answer *"Why does goodbye feel heavier when nothing was said?"*

When I reached the restaurant, I saw him already waiting back straight, hands folded on the table, coffee steaming in front of him. There was something achingly familiar about his stillness.

Aditya looked up, and I noticed how his face changed when he saw me, not dramatically, but just enough. His eyes softened; his shoulders loosened. I wondered if he realized how easy it was to read him.

I wanted to tell him that I would miss this, his calm, his quiet humor, the way he made silence feel comfortable instead of suffocating. But I didn't.

Instead, I smiled and said, "You're early."

The conversation began like a dance, one careful step at a time. We spoke regarding office, weather, our upcoming transfers. Safe things. Predictable things.
But every sentence had an unspoken echo trailing behind it.

When he told me that he was moving to Delhi, something inside me sank a little.
It shouldn't have. I'm leaving too. But knowing he wouldn't be here after I leave, that stung.

I had imagined him here for a long time, walking the same streets, sipping the same coffee, living the same life that still had traces of me. Now, even that small comfort was gone.

"Good for you," I said, forcing a smile. But my heart whispered, *"Don't go."*

**Aditya**

The waiter came, smiling politely, notebook ready. She ordered Roti and panner curry. I followed suit, because choices felt meaningless now.

"Same order as last time?" she asked, half-teasing. "Some things don't change," I said.
She looked at me, and for a second, it seemed like she wanted to ask *and some do?*

Instead, she said, "Do you remember that night we got drenched in the rain?"
"Of course," I said, smiling. "You blamed me for not carrying an umbrella."
"You said Bangaloreans don't need umbrellas." "I stand by that."
"Bangaloreans also get fevers," she said, laughing softly.

The laughter was short-lived but warm. It reminded me of what we used to be, two people orbiting each other, too scared to collide.

After the waiter left, I said, "You'll like Mumbai." She shrugged. "I don't know. Maybe. I'll try to."

"You'll write more there."

"Maybe."

"Maybe seems to be our favorite word," I said.

That made her smile. It was a small, knowing smile one that said she understood exactly what I meant.

**Mira**

He was trying too hard to sound fine. I could tell. He did that thing with his hands again rubbing his thumb against his wrist when he was nervous. Every time he looked at me, he looked away too quickly, as though afraid of being caught.

I wanted to reach across the table, touch his wrist, tell him, *"You don't have to pretend."* But I didn't. Because I was pretending too.

When he mentioned Delhi, I imagined him there surrounded by cold winters, foggy mornings, extreme summer, and people who didn't know how he took his coffee. The thought made a chest ache.

I'd told myself for weeks that I would move on, that Bangalore was just a phase, that he was just someone I met between metro stops and rain showers.
But sitting there, watching him stir sugar into his coffee like it was a ritual, I realized I'd been lying.

When the food arrived, we both thanked the waiter at the same time. our voices overlapped, and for a second, I felt the spark of something I'd almost forgotten, the rhythm of two people accidentally in sync.

I wanted to say it then, the truth I'd been carrying. But fear, that old friend of the heart, held me back again.

**Aditya**

Dinner ended quietly. We lingered long after the plates were cleared, pretending there was still something left to say.

"Should we get dessert?" she asked.

"Only if I'm paying," I said.

"You paid last time." "That's why I'm asking again."

She laughed, shaking her head. “You never change.” “You say that like it’s a bad thing.”

Her eyes softened. “Maybe it isn’t.”

We ordered one dessert a slice of chocolate cake to share. She took the first bite, then handed me the spoon. It felt oddly symbolic that our last shared moment was something sweet we didn’t finish.

When we finally stepped outside, the night air was cool and fragrant. A drizzle had just started, fine and hesitant.

She opened her umbrella; I didn’t. “Some things never change,” she said, echoing my earlier words. “Some shouldn’t,” I said.

We stood there, inches apart, both pretending not to notice how close we were.

“Mira,” I said, voice lower than a whisper. She turned, eyes shining with the kind of light that doesn’t come from reflections but from emotion.

But the moment passed. The rain grew heavier. And words like us found their own way to dissolve.

Outside the restaurant, the streetlights threw trembling circles on the wet pavement. I walked beside her in that half-rain that Bangalore does so well, too gentle to open an umbrella, too heavy to ignore. Cars hissed past. A child somewhere laughed. I was aware only of the sound of her sandals tapping a rhythm that matched my heartbeat.

We didn’t speak for a long time. There was nothing left that words could do. Everything that needed saying hung somewhere between the sound of the drizzle and the smell of filter coffee still on her sleeve.

At the crossing I said, “Let’s go by the lake. It’s quieter there.” She nodded.

We walked the narrow road toward Ulsoor. The reflections of neon signs floated on the puddles like broken constellations. I kept thinking: *This is what memory will look like blurred, glowing, impossible to hold still.*

"Do you remember," I asked finally, "the first day we met in the metro?" She smiled. "You mean when I dropped my notebook? I thought you'd never return it."
"I almost didn't. I kept it a day longer than I should have."

"Why?"

"I wanted to read what was inside."

"You did?"

I shook my head. "No. I was afraid it might end the mystery."

Her laugh was soft, and it carried over the sound of rain touching the water.

**Mira**

I was glad he hadn't read the notebook fully. Inside were pieces of mine he would never have understood then lists, half-finished poems, the word *stay* written more times than I cared to admit.

Walking beside him now, I could feel the same comfort that had always undone me. He never demanded words. He simply *was.*

The lake spread out to our left, still and silver. I watched the ripples made by falling rain and thought, *this is what our story looks like quiet disturbance over something deep.*

He kept glancing at me, maybe searching for permission to speak, maybe afraid of what would happen if he did. I wished he would say it, the thing I already knew, so that I wouldn't have to.

Instead, I said, "Delhi will suit you. You like space."

"And you," he replied, "belong somewhere with sound. Mumbai will love you."
I smiled but felt the ache rise behind my ribs.

**Aditya**

I wanted to tell her that I didn't want *space*; I wanted *presence.* But I said nothing.

We stopped under the old Gul mohar tree the same one that used to drop bright orange petals on the footpath during summer. The petals were gone now, replaced by small, wet leaves sticking to our shoes.

She brushed one from her kurta. "You always look at the sky when you talk," she said.

"Habit."

"Trying to find answers there?"

"Maybe I just don't want to miss the rain."

She laughed, but her eyes glistened. For a heartbeat, she looked exactly like she had the night we'd waited out the storm together under a broken roof, half wet, half laughing, all alive.

**Mira**

When he looked up, I looked at him. His face in the dim light was a map of things I hadn't read yet. I wanted to memorize it, so that years later, in some other city, I could trace it in my mind and still feel the calm of this night.

He said something then something ordinary about work, but I barely heard it. All I could hear was the sound of my own pulse and the single sentence I kept rehearsing: *"I love you."* It trembled behind my teeth, waiting.

But fear arrived first. Fear of being wrong, of ruining something sacred by naming it. So! I smiled instead and let the sentence dissolve. I don't wanted to break his friendship and how he is being with me.

**Aditya**

We walked until the rain thinned to mist. At a tea stall near the corner, I stopped.
"Coffee?" I asked.

"Always," she said.

We stood under the little awning while the man poured steaming filter coffee into steel tumblers. The aroma wrapped around us like memory.

"Do you remember," she said, "when you said you'd take me to the best coffee in Bangalore?"
"I still owe you that."

She lifted the cup. "Then let's call this it."

For a moment we just sipped, the steam fogging the small space between us. I wanted to reach for her hand; instead, I reached for my wallet.

**Mira**

I watched him fumble for change, noticed the tiny crease between his brows. Everything about him was careful; how he folded his napkin, how he said goodbye. I wondered what it would take for him to *not* be careful. To just reach out.

When he handed the vendor a note, our fingers brushed. A small, electric contact, too quick to be intentional, too real to be ignored. I drew back, heart thudding, and said, "We should go. It's late."

He nodded, eyes unreadable.

**Aditya**

We started walking back toward her lane. The silence between us was warm now, not heavy. It felt like a hand resting quietly on my shoulder. I realized then that love didn't always need confession. Sometimes it was enough to walk beside someone and know they were choosing the same direction, even if only for a little while.

We stood by the edge of the road, neither ready to say goodbye first.

"So, this is it?" I asked finally.

She nodded. "For now."

"For now," I repeated, as though saying it might make it true.

There was a moment, a heartbeat of possibility, when our hands brushed as we both reached for the umbrella handle. She looked at me, eyes glistening, and I thought maybe, maybe she feels it too.

But she stepped back first. "Goodnight, Aditya."

"Goodnight, Mira."

As she walked away, her reflection shimmered in the puddles, breaking with each step she took.

And just like that, she was gone leaving behind the echo of rain, and the silence of everything unspoken.

***

**Mira**

His scent still lingered on my dupatta, a trace of rain and coffee. I wanted to open the door again, to call him back, to say the words that pressed at my chest.

But I didn't. I simply whispered them into the dark: "I love you too."

That night after going home, I found myself writing without thinking. The words came like confession:

*There was a man who walked beside me.*

*He never said he loved me.*

*I never asked him to.*

*But we walked, and that was enough.*

I closed the notebook and smiled through the tears. Somewhere, I hoped, he was still walking too.

Then I wiped the tears, packed another box, and went back to my list of things to do before leaving Bangalore. I added one more line at the bottom, in hurried handwriting:

☐ Remember the walk.

# Search

---

*4 Years Later - Present*

---

Delhi's evening sky was a shade of bruised purple, the kind that suggested a storm had passed but left its memory behind. Aditya stood near his apartment window, watching the blurred silhouettes of people below. His reflection stared back from the glass tired, guilty, but finally awake.

For years, he had lived with the ghost of what he didn't say. Now, after hearing Ramya's words, after realizing Mira had once loved him, the weight had become unbearable. The silence that had once been his comfort now burned like regret.

He picked up his phone. There was only one person he needed to talk to: Aditi.

They met at their usual café, a quiet place tucked behind a line of bookshops in South Delhi. The faint aroma of roasted beans hung in the air, mingling with the soft hum of indie music. Aditi was already there, sitting by the window, her hair tied up loosely, a book open in front of her.

When she looked up and saw him, she smiled, though there was hesitation behind it. "You came."

Aditya nodded. "I had to."

He sat down, the words forming heavy knots in his throat. For once, he didn't want to delay what needed to be said.

"I need to tell you something," he began, his voice low. "And it's not easy."

Aditi closed her book gently, sensing the weight in his tone. "About her?" she asked softly.

He nodded.

She leaned back, waiting.

Aditya's fingers traced the rim of his coffee cup as he spoke. "Four years ago, there was someone... Mira. We were close. We walked together almost every evening in Bangalore. I thought it was just friendship, but it wasn't. I loved her, I just never said it."

Aditi's eyes didn't leave his. There was no flicker of surprise only quiet comprehension.

He continued, each word pulled out like a confession to himself. "By the time I realized what she meant to me, she was gone. She moved to Mumbai. I didn't stop her. I didn't even try. I told myself it was fine, that life moves on. But it never really did."

For a while, Aditi said nothing. The world outside moved, horns blaring, the evening rush growing, but inside the café, time felt suspended.

Finally, she asked, "Do you still love her?"

Aditya hesitated. His instinct was to deny, to make things simpler. But that wasn't what Aditi deserved. She had been nothing but kind to him, patient even when he offered only fragments of himself.

"I don't know," he said truthfully. "But I think I need to find her, not just to know if she's still there, but to know who I was with her. Maybe I owe her that. Maybe I owe myself that."

Aditi looked down at her hands. When she spoke, her voice was calm, but her eyes glistened slightly. "You know what I like about you, Aditya?"

He frowned. "What?"

"You're finally being honest, maybe for the first time since I met you."

That caught him off guard. She smiled faintly. "Go. Find her. You should. Because if you don't, you'll always wonder what could have been. And you'll keep standing still halfway between your past and your present."

He felt a lump form in his throat. "Aditi, I don't want to hurt you."

She reached across the table, placing her hand over his. "You already have," she said gently. "But it's okay. It's not the kind that breaks you; it's the kind that teaches you."

After a moment, she added, "If you find her and she's still waiting then maybe that's your story. And if she's moved on, or you realize you've changed… then maybe come back and tell me. I might still be here. Or maybe I won't. But either way, we'll both know where we stand."

Her words carried no bitterness, only quiet strength the kind that comes from loving someone without trying to own them.

Aditya looked at her, searching for something to say, but words failed him. All he could manage was a quiet, "Thank you."

Aditi smiled faintly, withdrawing her hand. "Don't thank me. Just make it worth it."

They left the café together. The night air had cooled, carrying the faint scent of rain-soaked earth. The streetlights glowed pale gold, and for a brief moment, their shadows walked side by side, two people at the edge of different stories.

When they reached her car, she turned to him. "You'll find her," she said softly. "And maybe, along the way, you'll find yourself too."

He nodded, trying to memorize the steadiness in her voice, the compassion in her gaze. "Goodnight, Aditi."

She smiled. "Goodnight, Aditya. And good luck."

As he walked back through the quiet lanes, Aditya felt something shift inside him. The guilt and uncertainty that had haunted him for years now began to change shape, not into peace yet, but into purpose.

He pulled out his phone, opened his messages, and scrolled until he found Ramya's contact. His fingers hovered, then typed a simple line:

"Ramya, it's Aditya. I need your help; it's about Mira."

He hit send, exhaled, and felt the faintest flicker of something new beneath the weight of old memories, hope.

Ramya replied the next morning.

Her message was brief, almost cautious:

"Aditya? Wow, it's been years. About Mira! let's meet. Some things are easier to talk about face to face."

He hesitated only for a second before typing,

"Sure. You choose the place."

Within minutes, she responded with a café location in Gurgaon, tucked near the DLF Cyber City stretch. It was the kind of place that thrived on nostalgia and soft music, much like the past he was about to revisit.

When Aditya arrived, Ramya was already there, camera slung across her shoulder, hair longer now, a little tired around the eyes but still carrying that confident energy.

"Aditya," she said with a half-smile, standing to greet him. "You look the same, since I met you! Sorry about our last meet"

He laughed softly, shaking her hand. "That's polite for 'you look tired.'"

She chuckled. "Maybe. But Delhi tends to do that to people."

They sat. Two cups of cappuccino arrived without them asking, and for a moment, neither spoke, both knowing why they were here, yet neither knowing where to begin.

Ramya broke the silence first. "So, you're really asking about Mira after all these years."

Aditya nodded slowly. "I know it sounds strange. But I've been… carrying her with me. I never said what I should have said, and now I just need to know how she is. Whether she's happy. Whether she's…" He trailed off, unable to finish the sentence.

Ramya leaned back, studying him. "You're still the quiet one, huh? Always thinking more than you say."

He smiled faintly. "Still guilty of that, yes."

She softened. "You know, when I met you in Bangalore that day at dinner, she talked about you before we went. She kept saying you were different not in some romantic cliché way, but like she could breathe around you. You gave her calm."

The words hit him like gentle blows each one reminding him what he'd lost by staying silent.

He took a breath. "Do you know where she is now?"

Ramya frowned slightly. "That's the thing. I don't, not exactly. She moved to Mumbai after that job offer, but she wasn't really in touch much afterward. The last I heard, she was working with a big publishing house, one of those well-known ones in Lower Parel. I think it was called… PaperLeaf or LeafLine. Something with 'leaf.'"

Aditya's mind latched onto the word like it was oxygen. *Leaf.*

"PaperLeaf?" he repeated. "That's the company, right?"

"Yes, I think so," Ramya said. "But that was three years ago. She changed her number after moving. I tried emailing her once, but no reply. Mira was always like that when she decided to move forward, she did it completely."

He nodded, processing. "Can you check if any of your old contacts in publishing still know her?"

Ramya nodded. “I can. I still freelance sometimes. I’ll reach out to a few editors I know maybe someone’s heard of her.”

For a while, they sat in comfortable silence.

Then Ramya said softly, “You know, when I met her after that dinner, she was quieter than usual. She said you hadn’t said anything. She didn’t blame you, she just said maybe it wasn’t meant to be.”

Aditya’s throat tightened. “It could have been.”

Ramya sighed. “Maybe. But life doesn’t wait for words, Aditya. It keeps moving.”

He stared into his coffee, the swirling foam reflecting faint gold light. “I just need to find her. Even if she’s moved on, I need to know.”

Ramya reached across the table, her tone firm now. “Then find her. But do it for the right reason. Not to fix the past, but to understand it. If you’re looking for closure, let it come gently.”

He met her eyes, grateful. “You sound like Mira sometimes.”

Ramya laughed softly. “Well, writers rub off on their friends.”

She opened her phone, quickly typing something. “I’ve texted a few people already. If I hear anything, I’ll let you know. In the meantime, try searching online. Mira never liked social media, but she had a blog once, maybe it’s still out there.”

He nodded. “I’ll check.”

They stood outside afterward, near the edge of the parking lot. The wind carried the faint hum of the city, horns, chatter, life.

Ramya smiled. “You know, I didn’t think I’d see you again. But maybe this is good. Maybe she needs someone looking for her.”

“Maybe,” he said quietly. “Or maybe I just need to find what I lost in myself.”

She gave a small, approving nod. “That’s what makes it worth it.”

As she walked away, camera swinging at her side, Aditya realized how much time had passed and yet how the past still had a way of catching up, breathing softly down his neck like a memory refusing to die.

That evening, back in his apartment, Aditya searched *PaperLeaf Publishing* on his laptop.

A clean, elegant website appeared filled with smiling author profiles, press releases, and glossy book covers. He scrolled slowly, eyes scanning for a familiar name.

Nothing.

But at the bottom of the staff page, in small print, he found something:

"Senior Editorial Team (2019–2020): Mira Patil"

His breath caught. There she was.

The company had updated their site recently, which meant she wasn't there anymore. But it was something. It was proof she had been there, that she existed beyond memory.

And for Aditya, that was enough to keep going.

***

It was nearly midnight when Aditya closed his laptop. The screen's glow had etched faint blue rings beneath his eyes. His search for *"Mira Patil PaperLeaf"* had yielded nothing new after hours of scrolling through archives, literary pages, and event photographs.

But he had caught her name once, just once, on an old article titled *"Emerging Voices in Indian Fiction"*. It was dated 2020, a brief mention:

"Editor Mira Patil of PaperLeaf believes every story deserves to find its reader."

He read the line over and over again, not because of what it said, but because he could hear her voice saying it, soft, deliberate, filled with conviction.

That was how she spoke when she believed in something.

Over the next days, Aditya's routine changed entirely. Mornings were mechanical - office work, meetings, client calls but as soon as he returned home, he dived into his search.

He checked LinkedIn, Facebook, Instagram, Twitter. Nothing. It was as if Mira had erased herself from the digital world.

He tried every variation *Mira P.*, *Mira Writes*, *Mira PaperLeaf*, *Patil Publishing*. Still, no trace.

Some profiles looked closely a photo that resembled her from a distance, a name with the same initials but every time he clicked, it wasn't her. Each disappointment cut deeper, like chasing shadows that vanished when he got too close.

When he could no longer bear the frustration, he turned to memory. He reopened an old folder on his laptop, *Bangalore Photos 2019*.

Most of the pictures were unremarkable: blurry sunsets, metro stations, half-eaten meals, random street corners. But each photo carried a ghost of her presence, a coffee cup opposite his at a café table, a scarf hanging loosely from a chair, the faint reflection of her face in a window's glass.

He hadn't realized how often he'd taken photos when she was nearby. It was as though his subconscious had been documenting what his heart refused to admit.

He stared at one picture, the rain-specked window of his old apartment, the faint outline of a woman's shadow walking past on the street below. He could almost hear her laugh in the distance.

Late one night, while searching her name alongside writing keywords, he stumbled upon something new, a WordPress blog titled *"The Fifth Season."*

The description read:

"For stories that belong to the space between rain and silence."

He froze.

That phrase *between rain and silence* was hers. He had heard her use it once when they were walking back from their usual route, rain drizzling gently. She had said, "Bangalore has a fifth season that time between rain and silence, when the city doesn't know what it wants to be."

He clicked on the blog.

The posts were dated sporadically 2019 to 2020 written under the name *M.P.*

Each entry was short, poetic, and deeply personal. They were written like open letters, full of imagery that made his chest tighten.

"Sometimes I still dream of a city that smells like coffee and Gul mohar trees. There, silence had a name, and it used to walk beside me."

He didn't need confirmation. It was her.

Line after line carried her rhythm, her pauses, her way of turning the mundane into something almost sacred.

And then, one post stopped him cold.

*"Maybe love is not about saying it. Maybe it's about walking quietly beside someone, knowing you could, but never needing to. Until one day, you do, and it's too late."*

He closed his eyes. He didn't cry. But something inside him cracked, quietly, like an old branch giving way under its own weight.

He sat for hours rereading the blog, tracing the emotional trail across years. The later posts hinted at change, a new city, deadlines, meetings, exhaustion, and a strange melancholy that crept into her tone.

*"Home isn't always a place. Sometimes, it's the version of yourself that someone once saw and loved."*

Was that about him? Or someone else?

He didn't know. But he wanted to.

For the first time in four years, he wanted to reach her not out of guilt but out of need. To know her truth, not his version of it.

He found the contact form on the blog, his fingers hovering over the keyboard.
He typed slowly:

*Hi Mira,*

*It's been a long time. I came across your writing. I don't know if you'll want to hear from me, but I hope you're doing well.*

*– Aditya.*

He read it twice. Then three times.

And then he sent it. He bookmarked the page, whispering to himself, "At least I found you."

When Aditya finally looked up, dawn was creeping into the city. The birds outside his balcony had started their scattered chorus. He stood there, watching the faint blush of sunlight spread across the Delhi skyline, and for the first time in years, his heart didn't feel empty.

It felt full, with uncertainty, yes, but also purpose.

Somewhere out there, Mira was living her life, writing her stories. And he wasn't lost anymore. He was following the trail she had unknowingly left behind.

***

Saturday morning came quietly. Delhi had one of those slow, sleepy weekends where sunlight slanted lazily through curtains, and time felt thicker.

Aditya sat on the floor beside his bed, an old hard drive connected to his laptop. He hadn't opened that drive in years, it contained fragments of his

Bangalore life: project files, photos, and random scans of things he never wanted to lose.

He wasn't sure why he opened it that morning. Maybe it was instinct, or maybe something Mira's blog had stirred inside him, a desire to hold something real again, not just digital echoes.

Among folders labeled *Work*, *Expenses*, and *Misc*, one caught his attention: *Mira – Notes*.

He clicked it. Inside were a handful of scanned images, quick photos he'd taken years ago, one evening in her presence. Her old brown notebook lay open on a café table, her handwriting looping across the page in blue ink. He remembered teasing her about her precise lettering, how she'd laughed and said, *"Writers are judged by their handwriting before their words."*

He opened the first image.

A poem stared back at him, untitled, but unforgettable. He still remembered the rhythm; she'd read it aloud once when the power had gone out, her voice the only light in the room.

*When it rains in this city, the trees listen first.*
*The people only notice when silence arrives after.*
*Somewhere, a window fogs with someone's waiting,*
*and the wind hums a name that never got spoken.*

It had been simple, but it had carried her entire essence, the tenderness, the restraint, the ache.

He had photographed that page because something in him knew he'd want to remember it someday.

Now, he stared at the image, tracing every word with his eyes until the text blurred.

Later that afternoon, as he scrolled through *PaperLeaf Publishing's* archives, one headline stopped him:

**"Anthology of Contemporary Indian Poetry (2023 Edition)"**

Curiosity made him click. The page loaded slowly, revealing the contributors' list, twenty-five names, some known, some obscure. Near the middle, one name caught his eye:

"Poem: The Wind Hums a Name – by Myra Sharma & M.P."

His heart lurched.

The title: *The Wind Hums a Name.*

Almost identical to her handwritten poem.

He clicked through, and when the text appeared on screen, he didn't need to finish reading it to know, it was the same poem. Line for line. Word for word.

Only the name had changed.

Not *Mira Patil.*

But Myra Sharma & M.P.

He leaned back, stunned. Was it her? Could it be a coincidence?

It wasn't unusual for writers to use pseudonyms especially if they wanted privacy, or to write without professional constraints. But "Myra Sharma" even the way the letters curved, even the rhythm of her name felt like her, like she had just shifted one syllable to hide in plain sight.

He searched *Myra Sharma PaperLeaf*, and sure enough, there were traces event mentions, small interviews, credits in obscure poetry platforms.

Everywhere he looked, the writing bore her cadence: that same quiet melancholy, the same pulse beneath the sentences.

*"Love doesn't end when people leave. It ends when the silence between them forgets the sound of their names."*

It was hers. No one else could have written that.

Aditya opened a spreadsheet he kept a simple timeline of what he knew.

- **2019:** Mira leaves Bangalore for Mumbai.

- **2019:** Works at PaperLeaf Publishing as Senior Editor.
- **2020:** Mentioned in literary article.
- **2023:** "Myra Sharma" publishes a poem in PaperLeaf's anthology along with M.P.
- **2023:** "The Fifth Season" blog posts end abruptly in May.

He stared at the pattern.

Why did it co-authored, along with someone? Or is Myra and Mira are same? Is she married to Sharma? But It's Myra not Mira, her last known publication, her final blog entry, both stopped around the same time. After that, nothing. As if she'd dissolved again into silence.

But now he knew she hadn't vanished entirely. She had simply become someone else; *Myra Sharma.*

And maybe, she had wanted to be found only by those who still remembered the old her. He sat in silence, the laptop screen glowing faintly in the dim light.

Four years ago, she had written that poem while sitting across from him, stirring her coffee slowly, speaking about how words often lived longer than people's courage.

He hadn't realized how true that would become. She had left, but her words had stayed and now they had led him back to her, like breadcrumbs scattered through time.

Aditya smiled faintly, a mix of relief and sorrow washing over him. "You're still writing," he whispered. "Still hiding in words."

For the first time in years, his heart didn't ache with absence. It pulsed with purpose. That night, he printed the poem. It felt like proof, proof that she had once existed beyond memory, that she was still somewhere out there, breathing, creating, living through her art.

He pinned the printed poem beside his desk, next to her scanned notebook page. The two versions handwritten and published sat side by side, like echoes across time finally finding each other.

He looked at them and said quietly, “All right, Mira. Myra. Whoever you are now. I’m coming to find you.”

And with that, he opened a new browser tab, searching for one thing:

“PaperLeaf Publishing Mumbai – Head Office Address.”

This time, he didn’t hesitate.

He bought a flight ticket to Mumbai for the weekend.

***

As he packed that night, Aditi’s words returned to him: *“If she’s still waiting, that’s your story. And if she’s not... maybe come back and tell me.”*

He smiled, a small, wistful curve of his lips. “I’ll find out soon enough.”

And for the first time in years, he slept deeply not because the ache was gone, but because it had finally found a direction.

# Mumbai

# Part - 3

# Mumbai

The flight touched down at Mumbai's Chhatrapati Shivaji International Airport a little past noon. The plane's tires screeched faintly on the runway, jolting me awake from a half-sleep of dreams I couldn't remember.

Through the small oval window, the city unfolded beneath a soft haze endless rows of concrete, glinting high-rises, narrow lanes shimmering in the afternoon heat. Mumbai. The city Mira had called home, the place where her story continued after mine had stopped.

I sat there for a long moment, watching baggage trucks crawl past on the tarmac, trying to calm the quiet storm inside me.

Four years. That was how long it had taken me to come here, not for work, not for escape, but for something closer to truth.

The humidity hit me the moment I stepped outside the terminal. It clung to my skin, heavy and salt-thick, carrying the scent of the nearby sea. I got into a taxi, the kind with seats covered in fading brown leather and a dashboard decorated with tiny idols of Ganesh and Sai Baba.

"Where to?" the driver asked, adjusting his rearview mirror.

"Juhu," I said. "Seaside Hotel."

He nodded, started the engine, and the car joined the chaos of Mumbai traffic honking horns, buses exhaling smoke, people crossing roads as if fear was a forgotten concept.

As we moved, the city pulsed around me a rhythm of movement and noise that was both overwhelming and strangely alive. Mira had once told me over coffee in Bangalore, *"You'd love Mumbai. It's a city that never lets you stay still — even sadness here has motion."*

I looked out the window and thought, *Maybe I'm ready for that motion now.*

The hotel wasn't luxurious, but it had a view, a wide expanse of beach stretching endlessly, the Arabian Sea churning under the late afternoon sun.

From my balcony, I could see children running barefoot along the sand, lovers walking hand in hand, vendors selling roasted corn under colorful umbrellas. The sound of waves mingled with distant laughter and the faint rhythm of film songs playing from somewhere nearby.

I dropped my bags and sat on the edge of the bed. For a long time, I just listened.

It was strange how cities carried their own music. Bangalore had been soft rain tapping on windows, the hum of metro lines, the whisper of trees. Mumbai was louder, sea waves, traffic, human voices blending into a constant, living heartbeat.

And somewhere in that noise, I imagined her Mira, walking down these same streets, her scarf fluttering, her notebook pressed against her chest.

As the sun dipped lower, I stepped out of the hotel. The beach stretched before me, golden in the dying light. The sea breeze was warm and tasted faintly of salt and fried snacks from nearby stalls.

People had begun gathering joggers, families, tourists. A group of kids chased a deflated football, shouting in Marathi and laughter.

I walked slowly along the shoreline, the water washing over my shoes, leaving behind soft impressions that the next wave immediately erased.

Every step felt heavy with memory. Bangalore had its own rhythm, but here, the sea seemed to breathe in time with my heart calm one second, crashing the next.

For the first time in years, I allowed myself to imagine what tomorrow could bring. I pictured myself walking into her office, seeing her again, her surprise, her smile.

I imagined her voice saying, *"Aditya? Is it really you?"* and my quiet answer: *"I told you I'd find you."*

The thought brought an unguarded smile to my face.

After dinner at a small South Indian restaurant tucked in one of Juhu's narrow lanes, I ordered a tumbler of filter coffee, the kind Mira used to love.

She had once told me, "If you ever visit Mumbai, promise me you'll try the filter coffee near the beach. It tastes different there sweeter, maybe because of the salt in the air."

I took my first sip. She had been right. It wasn't about the taste, it was about the memory it carried. The warmth of steel against my palm, the frothy top, the faint echo of her laughter.

For a brief second, it almost felt like she was sitting across from me again.

Back at the hotel, I stood by the window, watching the night spread across the city. The lights reflected on the sea like scattered stars.

Tomorrow. The word pulsed in my mind. Tomorrow, I would go to *PaperLeaf Publishing.* Tomorrow, I might finally see her the girl I never stopped carrying inside me.

I lay down, pulling the thin blanket over me. Sleep came quickly, tangled with hope.

I saw her again walking toward me in the PaperLeaf office, her hair slightly longer, her smile exactly as I remembered.

"Mira," I said.

She laughed, her eyes shining. "Aditya," she whispered, "you finally came."

When she hugged me, everything else disappeared the years, the distance, the silence.

“I love you, Aditya,” she said against my chest.

“I love you too, Mira,” I answered, my voice trembling.

The world blurred.

And then it was a dream.

I woke up.

The sunlight was sharp and real, pouring through the half-open curtains. The ceiling fan whirred softly above me.

The dream clung to me like perfume vivid, sweet, and already fading.

I sat up slowly, pressing a hand over my chest. “Let this come true,” I whispered to the empty room. “Just once.”

The clock read 8:10 a.m.

It was time to find her.

I left the hotel just after nine. The sun was already bright, but the sea breeze softened its sting. As I booked a cab toward Lower Parel, I couldn't help smiling the kind of smile that came uninvited, born out of quiet anticipation.

For the first time in years, I felt young again, almost nervous. I caught my reflection in the cab's rearview mirror, slightly unshaven, eyes faintly tired but alive.

“PaperLeaf Publishing,” I told the driver and gave the OTP.

He nodded and turned into the traffic, and the city began to move around me busy, chaotic, filled with the sound of horns and vendors calling out. But beneath the noise, I felt something else a hum, a rhythm, like the city itself was whispering, *You're close.*

PaperLeaf's Mumbai office stood in a narrow lane off the main road, a sleek glass building surrounded by bougainvillea and small cafés. The sign out front read *"PaperLeaf Publishing Pvt. Ltd."* in elegant serif letters.

As I stepped inside, cool air greeted me, the hum of air conditioning, faint typing noises, the quiet chatter of professionals deep in their routines.

Behind the reception desk, a young woman looked up from her screen, her expression polite and practiced.

"Good morning, sir. How can I help you?"

I smiled nervously. "Good morning. I'm here to meet someone or rather, to inquire about someone who used to work here. Her name was Mira Patil."

The receptionist's eyebrows furrowed slightly. "Mira… Patil?" She clicked rapidly on her computer, eyes scanning something on the monitor. "She used to work here a few years ago, I think."

"Yes," I said quickly. "I believe she was a senior editor here."

She nodded slowly. "One moment, sir. Please wait." She picked up the intercom and said softly, "Ma'am, there's someone here asking about Ms. Mira Patil. Should I send him up?"

A pause. Then a faint voice replied, "Yes, please. Bring him to my office."

She looked back at me. "You can go up to the third floor. The regional manager, Ms. Shah, would like to speak with you."

"Ms. Shah," I repeated, the name echoing oddly.

The elevator ride felt longer than it was. My heart was beating faster now not with fear, but something closer to awe. The possibility that I might see her again was so close I could almost taste it.

When the elevator doors opened, I stepped into a corridor lined with framed book covers and author photos. At the far end, an open door revealed a neatly arranged office with sunlight spilling across the desk. "Mr. Aditya?" a voice called softly.

I turned. A woman in her early forties stood near the desk, smiling gently. "I'm Yukta Shah, regional manager. Please, come in."

I sat across from her. The room smelled faintly of coffee and old paper. Behind her, a shelf overflowed with manuscripts and printed proofs.

"So, you were asking about Mira Patil?" she said, folding her hands.

"Yes," I said carefully. "We were… old friends. I just wanted to know how she's doing. It's been years since we met."

Ms. Shah's expression softened in a way that immediately made my stomach tighten.

"I see," she said quietly. "You must have been close."

I nodded; my throat suddenly dry. "We were. I lost touch with her when she moved to Mumbai. I recently found some of her published work, poems, essays and I thought maybe I could find her here."

Ms. Shah looked down for a moment, then back at me. Her tone changed slightly, softer, slower.

"Mr. Aditya… Mira was with us until 2020."

The word *was* hung in the air like a slow echo.

"She's… not here anymore?" I asked, though I already felt the ground shifting beneath me.

Ms. Shah's eyes held mine, filled with a sympathy I wasn't prepared for.

"She passed away during the first wave of COVID," she said softly. "It was… it was a terrible time. We lost many people from our team, but Mira's loss was felt deeply. She was special, gentle, talented, kind. We all loved her here."

I couldn't breathe. For a moment, everything blurred, the room, the sound of the air conditioner, her voice.

My hands clenched on my knees, the air thick in my throat. "No," I said quietly, almost to myself. "That can't be."

Ms. Shah looked down again, her voice barely above a whisper. "She was hospitalized for a few days, but… things worsened very suddenly. Her parents were here in Mumbai; they handled everything privately."

I sat there, frozen. It felt like someone had pulled the world out from under me.

She had been here in this very building, maybe in this very room, working, laughing, breathing. And now she was gone.

The Mira I had been chasing through years of memory, poetry, and silence gone, long before I had even begun my search.

Ms. Shah hesitated, then added gently, "You knew her well?"

I swallowed hard, nodding. "I thought I did."

For a long moment, neither of us spoke. The sound of distant typing floated faintly through the half-open door.

When I finally found my voice, it came out as a whisper. "I saw her poem published under the name Myra Sharma. That was hers, right?"

Ms. Shah looked surprised, then smiled faintly. "Ah, yes. That was one of her closest friends Myra Sharma. They worked together. Mira used to help edit her poems before she passed. They were almost inseparable."

She paused, thinking. "You could get in touch with Myra, if you want. She was deeply affected by Mira's loss. Maybe she could tell you more. I still have her contact somewhere."

She scribbled a number on a sticky note and slid it across the desk.

I took it, staring at the digits as if they were a code to another life.

"Thank you," I said quietly.

Ms. Shah gave me a small, kind smile. "Mira spoke fondly of someone named Aditya once," she said softly. "Now I understand."

I left the building in silence. The city outside was loud, alive, indifferent. The sun blazed off the pavement, and the sound of horns felt distant, almost muffled.

I stood by the roadside for a long time, holding the sticky note in my hand.

She was gone.

All this time, I had imagined reunion, laughter, forgiveness, closure. But all I found was absence, a silence that even the sea couldn't fill.

Somewhere, in a hospital room during those terrible months, she had fought for breath, and I had been miles away, thinking she was still writing, still living.

I pressed the note gently against my chest, whispering, "I found you too late, Mira."

The sea wind carried her name away.

# The Unsaid - Poems

I don't remember leaving the office. One minute, I was thanking Ms. Shah; the next, I was outside, the city's noise pressing in like a wave I couldn't hear. My steps were automatic one after another, the body moving while the mind lagged far behind.

The sunlight had grown harsher. It fell on everything: glass towers, street vendors, a man selling sugarcane juice, yet it all looked unreal, as if the world had turned into a film reel running without sound.

Mira. Gone.

The word *gone* felt inadequate, too small to contain what I was feeling.

I found myself walking aimlessly down a busy street, my hands trembling slightly. Somewhere nearby, the faint smell of roasted peanuts mingled with the metallic tang of rain on pavement. The scent hit something deep in me an echo of Bangalore evenings, of walks under drizzles and jasmine.

But there would be no "Let's Walk?" text now. No smile from across the lane. No voice calling my name.

The city blurred as I moved.

By the time I reached Marine Drive, the sky had begun to shift blue melting into grey, the sea restless beneath the wind.

I sat on the low concrete wall, facing the waves. Couples walked past, their laughter mingling with the cry of seagulls. Joggers passed in steady rhythm, headphones in, detached from everything except their heartbeat.

Tears started flowing like a river, unstoppable.

And there I was a man who had come across hundreds of miles chasing a memory, only to find a silence that would never answer back.

I leaned forward, elbows on my knees, and stared at the endless stretch of water.

The sea was never still, it roared, it whispered, it collided with itself. Mira had once said that cities by the sea were full of ghosts because the waves carried all the unsaid words people had thrown into them.

I thought about what I would throw in now.

Regret? Maybe. Love? Definitely.

I closed my eyes and imagined her standing beside me, the breeze pulling at her hair. She would have smiled and said something simple, something like, *"You finally came."*

And maybe, that would've been enough.

***

When the evening lights flickered on, I looked down at the sticky note still in my pocket. *Myra Sharma.*

The name felt strange on my tongue.

I didn't want to call. I didn't want to hear any more endings. But the silence around me was unbearable. So, I unlocked my phone, typed in the number, and pressed "Call."

It rang once. Twice.

Then a voice, warm, older, cautious. "Hello?"

"Hi… is this, Myra Sharma?"

"Yes. Who's this?"

"My name is Aditya," I said, trying to keep my tone steady. "I… I got your number from Ms. Shah at PaperLeaf. She mentioned you were close to Mira Patil."

The line went silent for a few seconds. Then, softly "You knew Mira? Are you Aditya?"

"Yes," I said quietly. "From Bangalore. We were… friends."

I could hear her sigh, the kind that carried both recognition and sadness.

"She spoke about you," Myra said finally. "Many times."

My heart stopped.

"She did?"

"Yes. She said you were one of the few people who understood silence."

We decided to meet that evening at a café near Bandra, close to Carter Road. I almost didn't go. But something about Myra's voice, calm, steady, full of something unspoken pulled me there.

The café was small, warm-lit, with wooden chairs and the smell of cinnamon coffee. I arrived early and sat near the window. Outside, the rain had begun again soft, hesitant drops that streaked the glass.

When she arrived, I recognized her immediately not from memory, but from resemblance. There was something of Mira in her not in face or form, but in presence. The same grounded gentleness.

"You must be Aditya," she said, sitting down. "Mira showed me your photo once from a metro ride, I think. You were both laughing."

I didn't remember her taking that picture, but suddenly I could see it, the reflection of two faces in a metro window, hers smiling, mine half-turned toward her.

"Yes," I said softly. "That was us."

For a while, we just talked. About nothing and everything! the city, work, books. Then, slowly, Myra began telling me about Mira's last years.

"She moved to Mumbai after PaperLeaf offered her a position," she said. "She loved the job. She was quiet, but her ideas carried weight. Everyone respected her."

I smiled faintly. "That sounds like her."

Myra nodded. "She never liked talking much about herself. But when she did, it was always about Bangalore her walks, the metro rides, the quiet evenings. And this one person she used to walk with."

She looked at me, her expression soft.

"She told me once that you made silence feel safe."

Something in my chest broke open. I couldn't speak for a long moment.

Myra continued, her voice careful. "When COVID hit, she kept working from home. She even started a small blog for her poetry again. But then she fell ill… and things got bad quickly. I was in touch with her till the last few days."

She paused, looking down at her cup. "She told me that if she recovered, she'd go to Bangalore again. There was someone she needed to tell something to."

The world tilted slightly.

I leaned back, staring out the rain-speckled window. "I should've gone to her," I whispered. "I kept waiting for the right time, the right words. But I think she was waiting too."

Myra reached across the table, resting her hand lightly on mine. "She never blamed you, Aditya. She was grateful for you. Even till the end." I started releasing her poems, to reach out to you, I succeed now.

I closed my eyes, swallowing hard. Gratitude was a beautiful word but not the one I had wanted.

"I thought I'd find her here," I said finally. "I thought I could… start again."

Myra smiled gently, her eyes glistening. "Maybe you still can, not with her, but through her."

Before we left, she handed me a small brown envelope when she was critical. “I kept some of her things. Her parents didn’t want to go through them. I think this belongs to you.”

I opened it slightly inside was a folded sheet of paper, yellowed at the edges.

Her handwriting. Mira’s unmistakable loops of blue ink.

*If ever I can’t say it out loud, know that silence was never emptiness. It was everything I couldn’t find the courage to speak.*

At the bottom, a tiny line:

— *For A.*

I traced the words slowly. My throat burned.

“Thank you,” I whispered.

Myra nodded. “She would’ve wanted you to have it.”

Later that night, I walked again by the beach near Juhu. The tide was high, waves crashing violently against the shore. The sky was moonless, but the sea glimmered faintly under the city lights.

I sat on the same bench I’d been at the previous night, holding Mira’s note in my hand.

There was no closure. There never would be. But there was presence; the undeniable, enduring echo of her.

Some loves don’t end. They just change form.

I whispered her name to the wind, half-hoping she might hear it somewhere beyond the horizon.

“Mira.”

The waves answered back in their endless language, the same rhythm we had once shared, walking side by side in another city, another lifetime.

And for the first time since learning she was gone, I smiled. Not because the pain had faded, but because she had lived beautifully enough to still move me, even now.

***

The next morning, the city woke before I did.

Through the hotel window, I could already hear the murmur outside, the clang of metal shutters rising, and the faint chorus of seagulls above the water. Mumbai was a city that didn't know how to pause and maybe that was its secret: it healed by moving.

I sat up slowly, the small brown envelope still lying on the bedside table. Mira's note peeked from its edge, the paper faintly crumpled, the ink slightly faded — but the words still alive.

*"Silence was never emptiness. It was everything I couldn't find the courage to speak."*

I read it again and again, as if repetition could make her voice real.

Downstairs, the café in the hotel lobby smelled of toast, butter, and freshly brewed coffee.

I ordered a tumbler of filter coffee again her coffee. The waiter poured it from the steel jug into the small glass with practiced rhythm, the aroma rising in gentle spirals.

As I took the first sip, I realized it wasn't just the taste that made this coffee hers, it was the memory of how she held the cup, how she blew softly before sipping, how she once said, *"It's strange, coffee can't talk, but it understands you better than most people."*

I smiled faintly, feeling something loosens inside my chest.

Maybe that was what love was, not the grand moments, but the quiet rituals we leave behind for others to rediscover.

After breakfast, I took a cab toward Colaba Causeway. I had no destination, I just needed to walk.

The street buzzed with life: vendors selling scarves and books, tourists bargaining in multiple languages, the smell of sea salt mixing with frying samosas.

Every corner of this city seemed to pulse with contradiction beauty tangled with chaos; order wrapped in noise.

Mira had loved that. She once wrote that Mumbai reminded her of a book left open, incomplete but endlessly alive.

I paused at a roadside bookstall, my eyes catching on a familiar cover: *"The Fifth Season — A Collection of Poems."*

Her anthology. The one that had stopped after May 2023.

I picked it up, flipping through its pages until I found her poem — *"The Wind Hums a Name."* I ran my fingers over the print, as though touch could bridge years.

The vendor looked at me and smiled. "That one sells well," he said. "People say it feels personal."

I nodded, unable to speak. "It does," I whispered. "It really does."

***

By afternoon, I found myself back at Marine Drive. The sea had become a part of my rhythm now a constant mirror.

I sat on the same stone ledge where I'd sat yesterday, holding her book open, reading each line slowly, letting it wash through me.

She had written of waves and waiting, of unfinished conversations, of silence that wasn't defeat but devotion.

Each word felt like a message smuggled across time, addressed directly to me.

I realized then that love the kind we shared never truly ended. It didn't disappear with distance or death. It simply changed its form, moving from presence to memory, from voice to ink.

And if love could transform, maybe so could I.

That evening, I went back to *PaperLeaf Publishing*. Ms. Shah seemed surprised to see me.

"I wanted to thank you," I told her. "For everything, for telling me the truth."

She smiled kindly. "I'm glad you met Myra. She's still working on a tribute project for Mira, an anthology of her unpublished poems. She could use your help, you know."

Something in her words flickered like a light switch.

I blinked. "Her poems? You still have them?"

"Yes. She used to email them to herself and to Myra. There's quite a collection. Myra's been trying to put them together for months, but she said it felt incomplete, like a story waiting for its other voice."

I stood there, the realization settling in slowly. Maybe *that* was my reason for coming. Not just to find her, but to finish what she had left behind.

Later that night, I met Myra again at a small writer's café near Carter Road. She brought a thick folder with her pages neatly bound the title handwritten in blue ink: *"The Unsaid — Poems by Mira Patil."*

I stared at the words for a long time.

"This was the title she wanted?" I asked softly.

Myra nodded. "Yes. She said that everything worth feeling usually stays unsaid."

I smiled through the ache. "That sounds like her."

We went through the pages together, her handwriting, her revisions, her digital drafts. Some were raw; others polished. But each one carried that same pulse, the quiet melancholy that made her voice unforgettable.

As I read, I began marking small notes in the margins, suggesting order, flow, themes just as she once used to do for her authors.

Myra watched me for a while, then said quietly, “You’re doing what she would’ve wanted.”

Two weeks later, the project was ready *The Unsaid*, an anthology of Mira’s final poems.

On the dedication page, I wrote:

*For Mira who taught me that silence has its own language, and that some loves don’t need endings to be complete.*

Myra read it, tears in her eyes. “She would’ve loved this.”

“I hope so,” I said softly. “Because I finally do.”

When the anthology released online, the response was immediate hundreds of readers sharing her words, quoting her lines, speaking of how deeply they resonated.

Her name *Mira Patil* began appearing again, not as a memory, but as a living voice. Myra told this time, it will be published under her name only, not with a co-author.

Every time I saw her poem shared by a stranger; I smiled. She was still here, whispering through others.

And somewhere in the back of my mind, I could hear her say, *“See, Aditya? Words outlive us all.”*

***

On my final evening in Mumbai, I went for one last walk by the sea.

The sun was low, painting the water in gold and rust. The air smelled of salt and roasted peanuts. The city’s hum was quieter somehow, as if pausing to listen.

I took off my shoes and walked along the wet sand, the waves curling around my feet.

There was no destination, no waiting figure, no text that would say *“Let’s Walk?”* but there was peace.

And in that peace, she was everywhere in the wind, the sound of the tide, the rhythm of the world itself.

I stopped near a stretch of rocks where the water broke hardest. I took out her note, now slightly wrinkled, and read it one last time.

*If ever I can't say it out loud, know that silence was never emptiness. It was everything I couldn't find the courage to speak.*

The paper trembled in my hands, caught by the wind.

"I heard you, Mira," I whispered. "I finally did."

I let the note go.

The wind caught it, lifting it gently, carrying it over the sea until it vanished into the horizon.

For a moment, I just stood there, letting the sound of the waves fill everything that words never could.

When I boarded my flight back to Delhi two days later, I felt lighter not because I had found her, but because I had finally understood her.

Some love stories don't need to end in togetherness. Some exist simply to change who we are.

As the plane ascended, the city receded beneath a haze of gold and silver. I looked down one last time, whispering, "Goodbye, Mira."

But deep down, I knew, it wasn't goodbye.

It was, finally, peace.

# Full Circle

The flight to Delhi felt longer than the one that had brought me to Mumbai. Maybe it was because I wasn't bringing hope back with me this time just the weight of truth.

As the aircraft rose above the Arabian Sea, I looked down one last time at the shimmering line where water met sky. Somewhere below that horizon lay all the words I hadn't said, all the moments I'd lost.

Mira's city grew smaller, swallowed by clouds, and I whispered quietly to myself, "Goodbye again."

The seatbelt light blinked, and I closed my eyes, letting exhaustion settle in. But sleep didn't come easy only flashes of her smile, her laugh, and her message that never reached me.

*Let's walk?*

Even in silence, it still echoed.

Delhi greeted me with a cold wind. The season had shifted a sharpness in the air, trees beginning to shed their leaves. The drive from the airport to my flat was quiet, the city flashing past in fragments, streetlights, traffic signals, people hurrying home.

Everything looked the same, yet I felt utterly misplaced, as if I had returned to a version of my life that no longer fit.

I dropped my bags on the couch and stood by the window. Outside, the skyline was a soft blur of fog and headlights. I could hear distant laughter from the neighboring apartments, the hum of life continuing as usual.

And yet, for me, everything had stopped the moment I heard *"Mira is no more."*

Aditi called that evening. Her voice was as warm as ever.

"Aditya? You're back?"

"Yes," I said softly.

"You sound… different. How was Mumbai?"

There was no easy answer to that. "Can we meet tomorrow?"

She paused, maybe sensing the heaviness behind my tone. "Of course. The usual café?"

"Yes. Ten a.m.?"

"Done."

When the call ended, I sat in the dark for a long time. I knew what I had to tell her, and I hated that it would hurt her.

The café was nearly empty when I arrived the next morning. The smell of roasted beans hung in the air. Aditi was already there, sitting by the window, her bright red scarf a splash of color against the grey morning.

She smiled when she saw me, but it faded quickly as she read my expression.

"You found her, didn't you?" she asked softly.

I nodded. "Yes."

She leaned forward, eyes searching mine. "And?"

I took a deep breath. "She's gonc, Aditi. Mira's no more."

Her hand froze around her cup. For a moment, neither of us spoke. The hum of the coffee machine filled the silence.

"Oh, Aditya…" she whispered finally. "I'm so sorry."

I nodded, unable to meet her eyes.

After a long pause, I said quietly, "There's something else I need to tell you."

Aditi nodded gently, waiting. "I met someone, her friend, Myra Sharma. She told me that the last message Mira ever got from me was 'Let's walk.' She wanted to reply… but she never did."

Aditi frowned slightly. "Why?"

"Because she heard from my cousin Rohit when he stayed with me in Bangalore that I was engaged. That there was someone else in my life."

Aditi's eyes widened. "But that's not true."

I shook my head. "No. But she believed it. She thought I had moved on. So, she stepped away quietly. She never knew that I was waiting too."

My voice cracked on the last word.

Aditi's gaze softened with sadness not jealousy, not anger, just quiet empathy. "That's… cruel, Aditya. That misunderstanding changed everything."

"Yes," I said, my voice breaking. "It did."

Aditi reached out, touching my hand. "You did everything you could. You found her, even if it was too late."

I shook my head. "No. I found her words, her echoes, but not her. I was too late and now I can't give my heart to anyone else. Not now. It wouldn't be right."

Her fingers tightened slightly around mine. "Are you saying what I think you're saying?"

I looked at her really looked. She was kind, beautiful, full of life. Someone who deserved certainty, not half-healed fragments.

"Aditi," I said gently, "I can't be in a relationship right now. It would be unjust to you. My heart still belongs somewhere else even if that person isn't here anymore."

Her eyes shimmered. "But you and I… we were starting something."

"I know," I said softly. "And you've been wonderful. But I'd be lying if I said I'm ready. I'm not."

She looked down, blinking fast. "I thought maybe I could help you heal."

"You already did," I whispered. "Just by being you."

We sat in silence for a long time. Finally, Aditi sighed, a small smile touching her lips through the tears.

"You're an impossible man, Aditya."

"Maybe," I said quietly. "But I don't want to hurt you by pretending."

She nodded, wiping her eyes. "I appreciate your honesty, even if it breaks my heart a little."

I reached across the table. "You'll find someone who deserves you, who can love you the way I couldn't."

She gave a soft laugh. "Don't make it sound so dramatic. Maybe one day you'll find peace too and maybe we'll meet again as different people."

"Maybe," I said.

We walked out together, the morning sun catching in her hair. At the corner where our paths split, she stopped and said, "Take care of yourself, Aditya. And of her memory."

"I will," I promised.

And then she was gone swallowed by the crowd, just like Mira once had been.

When I got back home, the apartment felt emptier than ever. The furniture seemed heavier, the air thicker.

I sat on the floor, Mira's notebook on the table beside me. I flipped through its pages, reading her lines once again:

*"Love doesn't fade when people leave. It fades when silence forgets their name."*

I whispered her name out loud, refusing to let silence win.

"Mira."

The word lingered in the still air like incense.

I knew what I had to do. Staying here in this city, in this room filled with ghosts would only trap me in circles. I needed to go back to where it all began. Back to the city that had once taught me how to walk beside her.

That night, I sent an email to my company. A simple request for transfer back to Bengaluru.

No explanations. No reasons. Just a single line in the message:

*"Returning back."*

When I hit send, something in me lifted not joy, not relief, but a quiet surrender.

I was going back. Not for closure, not to relive the past, but to keep it alive in the only way I knew through memory, through place.

Weeks later, I boarded the train south. I chose the train deliberately slower, longer, giving me time to think, to let the miles dissolve the ache bit by bit.

Outside, the landscape shifted gradually concrete giving way to fields, then to palm trees swaying against a pale sky. The rhythm of the wheels against the tracks felt almost like breathing.

Somewhere around dawn, as the train neared the city, I caught the faint smell of rain in the air. It felt like the city was welcoming me back.

Bengaluru, the place where I'd learned how to fall in love with quietness.

And now, maybe, how to live with it.

# Let's Walk

When the train finally pulled into Krantivira Sangolli Rayanna station, the city greeted me like an old friend who had aged quietly.

The air smelled the same: a mix of petrichor, and something unexplainably gentle. The skyline hadn't changed much either: the pale orange dawn spreading over tall glass towers, autos zipping past in their familiar rhythm, and somewhere in the distance, a dog barking against the silence.

It felt strange to be back. The last time I had walked these streets, I had been a different man one who still believed in timing, one who thought love would wait patiently until words caught up.

Now, I was older. Not just in years, but in understanding.

The cab ride to Ulsoor lake was quiet. Every turn, every lane carried a ghost of the past. The corner café where Mira once insisted, we stop for coffee. The metro line slicing through the city like an artery. The bougainvillea spilling over compound walls, stubborn and bright as ever.

When I reached my old apartment street, I just stood for a while. The houses looked smaller than I remembered. The same tree the Gul mohar she loved stood there, its branches heavy with red blossoms.

It was like nothing had changed. And yet, everything had.

The landlord recognized me instantly. "Aditya sir! After so long!" he said, smiling wide.

I smiled back. "Feels good to be back."

The apartment is vacant now, waiting like a paused story. Dust coated the shelves, and the walls smelled faintly of rain. The old window by the living room still creaked when I opened it, revealing the same street below, the street where we used to walk.

The world outside was alive: children cycling past, a milkman shouting, a street vendor arranging jasmine flowers.

And somewhere in all that noise, I could almost hear her voice again soft, teasing, *"Let's Walk?"*

The air thickened in my chest.

I unpacked slowly, placing Mira's notebook on the table near the window. The brown cover had worn edges now, but her handwriting inside was still as alive as ever.

This apartment, this notebook, this street they weren't just places. They were the last pieces of her still breathing in my world.

By evening, the rain returned the kind of soft drizzle that made everything shimmer. I stepped outside, wearing the same black jacket I used to wear during our walks. The streets glowed under the amber streetlights, puddles reflecting fragments of the world above. The city had changed in small ways. New cafés had replaced the old ones. The metro line had extended further. But the rhythm the hum of Bangalore evenings was still the same.

As I walked, I passed by the small park where she used to stop and smell the flowers. The benches were freshly painted, and a new swing had been added. But the quietness of the place was still familiar, that sacred silence we once shared.

I sat down for a moment, watching the raindrops fall through the glow of the lamps. In my mind, I could see her sitting beside me again, her hair damp, her laughter soft.

"Mira," I whispered, "you still live here, don't you?"

The breeze answered in rustling leaves.

As I stood up and began walking back, something caught my attention.

A few meters ahead, under a streetlight, a young couple stood. The girl wore a yellow kurta, holding her sandals in one hand. The boy beside her was smiling, hesitant.

Then he said it.

"Let's walk?"

My breath caught.

The girl laughed that same light, unguarded laugh that once belonged to another time and nodded. They started walking, side by side, the rain tracing their silhouettes in gold.

I froze.

It felt like watching a reflection of my own past, repeating gently in another lifetime.

Those two words so simple, so ordinary had once built a world for me. And now, hearing them again, it didn't hurt. It healed.

Because love, I realized, doesn't die with people. It lingers in gestures, in phrases, in small moments that keep replaying long after we're gone.

When I returned home, I left the window open. The city's night air drifted in, carrying the faint hum of rain and the fragrance of wet earth. I made myself a cup of filter coffee the ritual that had become my prayer and sat by the window, staring at the Gul mohar tree swaying gently outside.

Somewhere, a couple's laughter echoed faintly from the street. The world kept moving, as it should. I took a slow sip of coffee and opened Mira's notebook again. The last page was blank untouched.

I picked up a pen. For years, I had avoided writing anything in her book. But now, it felt right.

On that final page, I wrote:

*"You were right, Mira. Life always finds its way back to where it began.*

*The city still walks with your memory.*

*And I... I still walk with you."*

I paused, then added one last line.

*"Let's walk — always."*

The rain eased, and the moon slipped quietly between clouds.

I sat there for hours, letting the quiet fill the room. I didn't feel lonely anymore. The ache was still there, yes, but it wasn't emptiness, it was presence, soft and steady.

I realized that love isn't about having someone beside you. It's about carrying them within you, letting them shape how you see the world, how you move through it.

Outside, the street shimmered under the faint silver light. The young couple had disappeared down the lane, their laughter fading into the night.

I smiled.

Maybe that's how life works one story ending quietly while another begins with the same words.

As I closed the notebook, the power flickered briefly just like it used to during our walks when the city's lights would dim for a heartbeat before returning stronger.

The wind picked up, brushing against the curtains. I could almost hear her whisper again that same familiar, playful voice: *"Let's Walk?"*

And this time, I didn't hesitate.

I grabbed my umbrella and stepped outside.

The rain had stopped, but the streets were still wet, gleaming like memory itself. I walked with no destination, just letting my steps fall into rhythm with the city's pulse.

Somewhere behind me, the Gul mohar leaves shimmered under a passing breeze.

Each step felt lighter.

Each breath, easier.

I looked up at the night sky, smiling.

"Let's walk, Mira," I whispered. "One last time."

And I did through the same streets, under the same lights, with the same heart that had once waited in silence.

Back home, as I turned off the lights and let darkness settle, I realized the circle was complete.

Love had begun with a walk.

It had ended with one too.

And in between, there had been a life full of waiting, longing, discovery, and peace.

The silence in the room wasn't empty anymore. It was full, full of echoes, laughter, and everything that once was.

I closed my eyes, whispering one last time into the dark:

"Thank you, Mira… for walking with me."

-THE END-

Let's Walk by Mira Patil

# The Real - Mira

They say stories are born from memories that refuse to fade. Mine began with a walk and ended with one too.

But the story that the world read, the one people think belonged to Aditya, was always ours. Only, I had to tell it from his side because that's the only way I could keep him alive.

This isn't a confession.

It's a remembrance.

It's the truth the one hidden behind the silences and misunderstandings.

So here I am, Mira, standing under the soft yellow lights of my book launch in Mumbai, holding a copy of *"Let's Walk."*

The story of a man who waited.

The story of me, as told by him.

***

It was the same city Bengaluru.

The same metro, the same morning rush, the same smell of filter coffee that wrapped itself around you like an old memory.

And it was the same man.

I had noticed him long before he noticed me. Aditya: neat shirt, serious face, always with earphones plugged in, always staring outside the metro window as if searching for meaning in the blur.

He wasn't like most people I saw every day. There was something soft about the way he carried himself, like he didn't belong to the noise of the world. I used to watch him sometimes from a distance, our timings almost perfectly aligned MG Road station, 8:20 AM. Even in the evenings, I saw him way before he encountered me.

The first time we actually met or rather, when he *thought* we met was when I dropped my notebook. But it wasn't an accident.

I had seen his company ID card once, the blue lanyard swaying when he stood near the metro door. "Finstra Technologies," it read. And as fate would have it, my interview in the coming days was at the same company.

So yes, I dropped that notebook on purpose.

I wanted him to find it.

To have a reason to talk to me again.

That notebook had pieces of me, my to-do lists, my unfinished poems, my half-written thoughts about love and loneliness. When he picked it up, I knew he'd read it. I *wanted* him to.

It wasn't vanity. It was trust misplaced maybe, but pure.

And when I met him again in the street, pretending to be surprised, it felt like the universe had finally paused long enough for us to notice each other. Actually, I was waiting for three days for him to talk to me.

I never told him that I already knew. That when he handed it back, my heart had already begun to write chapters.

Those evenings in Ulsoor lake they were small, quiet miracles. He never said much. I didn't either. But silence with Aditya never felt like distance; it felt like home.

He would talk about his plants, his projects, his fascination with small details. I would listen, sometimes teasing him, sometimes just walking beside him in peaceful rhythm.

When it rained that day, and we stood together under the roof that's when I realized what was happening to me.

I wasn't just walking beside him anymore. I was falling beside him.

He never asked the company name where I had my interview. And I never told him. I thought it would be more beautiful as a surprise.

But destiny is strange.

That next day, when I walked into *his* office for the interview, his expression that mix of shock and delight said everything.

He didn't have to say it, but I knew he was happy I was there. And I… I was terrified of how happy that made me.

When I got the offer, I wanted to tell him immediately. But then life as it often does take a twist.

That evening, I had planned to meet him too. He had texted about dinner, and I knew, *I knew,* what it meant.

I had gone to the mall earlier that afternoon with Ramya. And that's when I saw him standing in front of the store, holding a small box. My heart had leapt.

He was buying a ring.

I had smiled like a fool, hiding behind a rack of scarves, watching him. After he left, I went inside and asked, pretending to be a random customer. "What did that man just buy?"

The saleswoman smiled and showed me a similar piece, an infinity ring. "Romantic choice," she said.

And for that one evening, I lived in a fairytale. I imagined him giving it to me, imagined myself saying yes, imagined everything.

But I never got that ring.

Because I took Ramya with me that night. She insisted we catch up, and I couldn't say no. I didn't know how to tell her that I was supposed to meet someone who made my heart race.

When Aditya saw me at the restaurant coming with Ramya, I saw his expression change. He smiled politely, but there was distance in his eyes.

And just like that, our moment slipped away.

A week later, I met his cousin, Rohit. He was funny, talkative, and unaware of how words can wound.

He told me casually, "My brother's getting some alliance proposals, I think. You know how families are. He's serious about someone, I guess."

I had smiled then, pretending it didn't matter. But inside, something broke. Because for days, Aditya hadn't spoken to me. The walks had stopped. The messages had stopped. And now, hearing this, it felt like a confirmation.

That ring was never meant for me. That silence wasn't hesitation. It was goodbye.

When Rohit asked about me, I said the same lie to protect my pride that I was moving to Mumbai, maybe even getting married soon.

We both lied to protect each other's hearts and ended up breaking them anyway.

I left the city with my notebook, my half-written poems, and an ache that refused to fade.

I was the girl in the red kurta outside the restaurant. Yes! the one he saw leaving as he entered inside the restaurant in Delhi. I saw him with Aditi, and I understood that he is moved on, but it wasn't 4 years later, it was after few months when I left for Mumbai.

Mumbai was louder, faster, harsher. But even here, on quiet evenings, I would still imagine him walking somewhere in Ulsoor lake maybe under that same Gul mohar tree, maybe still listening to his Kannada indie songs, maybe still waiting.

Then came the pandemic. And everything changed.

Just after few months, It was Ramya who told me. “Aditya…” she had said one evening over a shaky call, “he’s gone.”

The words didn’t register at first. “Gone where?”

She paused, her breath catching. “He didn’t make it through COVID.”

The room spun around me.

I couldn’t breathe. Couldn’t cry. Couldn’t accept that the person who once felt like home was now part of memory.

After he was gone, I began writing. Not as therapy, but as resurrection.

I wanted to imagine how *he* must have felt, the waiting, the confusion, the pain of unsaid love. I built his world from memory: His plants, his routines, his thoughts on marriage, his long metro rides. Everything I had once seen, now told through his eyes.

I made him live again, word by word, page by page.

And when I finished, I realized the book wasn’t just about him. It was about me too, about us, about what happens when two people love each other at the wrong time, in the right way.

***

Writing *Let’s Walk* took me two years. Not because I didn’t know what to say but because I was afraid of saying it.

Every page felt like reopening an old wound, letting the air sting before it healed again. There were nights when I’d stare at the blinking cursor, whispering, “What would you have said, Aditya?”

And sometimes, in the quiet between words, I could almost hear him that soft, thoughtful tone he used when speaking about life, how he saw meaning in mundane things.

Through him, I wrote about myself, but cleaner, braver, kinder. I wrote the Aditya I had known, and the Mira he had loved not perfect, but real.

I filled countless notebooks with fragments little dialogues from memory, metro rides, snippets of laughter that no longer echoed. And yet, every time I read them, I smiled.

It was as if I was walking beside him again.

One more metro ride.

One more shared silence.

One more chance to finish a story that real life never allowed us to complete.

Sometimes I'd imagine him editing my drafts, frowning over a sentence, muttering, "You could write this better."

Maybe that's why I could never move on because through writing, I never really had to say goodbye.

When *Let's Walk* was complete, I didn't write my name on the cover.

The world knew it as a debut novel by Myra *Sharma.* A pseudonym, yes! but one that carried both of us. "Myra" because it sounded like Mira, but also because it wasn't fully me.

The story was told from *his* point of view, but everything he said, every emotion he held back, every hesitation came from my understanding of him.

Readers called it *"a painfully honest portrayal of loneliness and connection."*

Some said, *"It's too intimate to be fiction."* They were right.

The book launch was held in Mumbai, at a small art café overlooking the sea. The evening sun melted into the horizon, staining the water gold.

People arrived editors, colleagues, friends. Cameras clicked, pages rustled, laughter filled the air. But all I could think about was how he would have hated such a crowd.

Aditya preferred quiet corners, not stages. He believed stories were personal, not performative. Still, I could feel him there in the breeze from the open door, in the smell of coffee, in the calm that always followed me when I thought of him.

When they called my name "Author Myra Sharma" I walked up to the small platform, my hands trembling slightly.

I looked at the book on the stand the same title written in clean white font: *Let's Walk.*

For a moment, I couldn't speak. My throat tightened. Then I smiled.

"Thank you all for being here," I began. "This book is special because it's not entirely fiction. It's about two people who met, and how silence became their third language. It's about love, not the kind that ends in togetherness, but the kind that never really ends at all."

After the reading, there was a small Q&A session. People asked about my writing process, the inspiration, the settings.

Then one woman, a young colleague from the publishing house, raised her hand. "Ma'am," she said with a curious smile, "how did you manage to write an entire story from a man's perspective so convincingly? The emotions, the loneliness, the thoughts it all feels so authentic. How did you do it?"

The hall went quiet.

I could feel every eye waiting for my answer.

I smiled softly, glancing down at the book in my hand. "It was easy," I said. "Because I imagined what he felt. I've known him, his silences, his fears, his way of thinking."

The girl nodded, still curious. "So, you researched men's emotions deeply?"

I shook my head. "No," I said, voice barely above a whisper. "It was easy for me because… I'm Mira."

The hall fell silent for a moment, then filled with a ripple of murmurs.

I smiled again, not to explain, but to remember.

Because that was all I needed to say.

After the event, people queued up for signatures. Each name I wrote felt like a piece of him, a memory passing through my hands.

Then a woman approached, one I didn't recognize. She wore a simple white saree, and her eyes were warm.

"You wrote this?" she asked softly.

"Yes," I smiled. "I did."

She looked at the cover and said, "It reminded me of someone I once knew. He used to talk about walking every evening, said it was his way of thinking clearly. His name was Aditya."

My heart clenched.

I managed a nod, forcing a smile. "Maybe it's the same one."

She looked at me for a moment as if recognizing something she couldn't quite place, then smiled back and walked away.

For the rest of the night, I couldn't stop thinking about that coincidence. Or maybe, it wasn't one.

When the event ended and the crowd thinned, I stood near the window overlooking the sea. The city lights reflected in the waves small, fleeting, beautiful.

I took a deep breath. The world outside was loud, but within me, everything was still. I could almost hear his voice, that steady calm, the way he used to say my name softly, as if afraid it would break.

"You did it, Mira," he whispered in memory.

And for the first time in years, I allowed myself to cry. Not in sadness, but in gratitude.

Because some love stories don't need a happily ever after, they just need to be told right.

After the launch, the days passed like slow-moving clouds. The buzz around the book grew interviews, reviews, mentions in magazines. People called it *"the most intimate story of modern love."*

But behind the applause, my days were quiet. I'd wake up early, make coffee, and sit by the balcony overlooking the sea. The mornings here had the same shade of blue as the sky in Bangalore. And sometimes, in the whisper of waves, I thought I could still hear his laugh.

I didn't write anything new. Not yet. *Let's Walk* had emptied me, not just as a writer, but as a person. It wasn't fiction anymore; it was everything I had carried for years.

Yet, the strange part of loss is that it doesn't end. It evolves. I wasn't haunted by Aditya's absence; I was accompanied by it.

One afternoon, I received a small parcel. No sender's name, just a familiar looping handwriting. Inside was a letter, and a small velvet box.

The letter began:

*"Dear Mira,*

*You don't know me, but I know about you. My name is Aditi. I was a friend of Aditya's or maybe something more, though never what he had with you. I found your name through a mutual friend in publishing. I hope this doesn't come as an intrusion."*

*"After he passed, some of his belongings were handed to me a few books, a ring box, and a worn-out notebook. I think he meant this for you. I thought it belonged to me once, but now I know, it never did."*

*"If love means holding someone in your thoughts long after they're gone, then I think you and I both loved the same man in different ways."*

*"This ring, it's yours. He never gave it to anyone. Maybe, in some small way, he was waiting for you."*

*With warmth,*

*Aditi."*

When I finished reading, my hands trembled.

I opened the small velvet box.

Inside lay the infinity ring.

Simple. Elegant. Endless.

The one I had once seen him buying in the mall.

For a long time, I couldn't move. The air seemed to thicken around me, as if the years between us were folding back into the present.

Tears came quietly not heavy or sharp, but gentle, like rain.

He had kept it all along.

That night, I wore the ring for the first time.

Not as a symbol of love unfulfilled, but of love remembered.

It fit perfectly as if it had been waiting all along.

Standing by the window, I whispered into the dark, "You kept it safe, Aditya. And now, I'll keep it safe for you."

I smiled faintly, remembering his habit of leaving mugs half full, his quiet way of smiling when he didn't know what to say.

For a moment, the world didn't feel lonely.

It felt full of him.

A few weeks later, I visited Aditi.

She lived in Delhi, a tidy apartment filled with plants, much like his old one.
She greeted me warmly, though there was a quiet tension between us not jealousy, but shared grief.

We spoke about him for hours.

"He talked about you often," Aditi said. "Not directly, but I could tell. The way his voice changed when he mentioned those Bangalore days."

I nodded, smiling faintly. "And I wrote about him every day. Maybe that's why we never really let him go."

Aditi looked at me, eyes soft. "He would've wanted this peace."

I reached across the table, took her hand. "Thank you for giving me the ring."

She smiled through her tears. "He would've wanted it with you. It belonged there all along."

That evening, when I left her house, the Delhi sky was painted orange. For the first time, I didn't feel the weight of distance.

We had both loved him and somehow, in sharing that love, we had both found closure.

Months later, when *Let's Walk* won a small literary award, I was asked to submit a short dedication for the ceremony brochure.

I kept it simple:

*"For Aditya who taught me how to see silence as a language. Some people walk beside you for a while, and some never stop walking with you, no matter where you go."*

When they read it aloud during the event, a quiet hush filled the room. I didn't cry. I smiled.

Because for the first time, it didn't hurt to remember.

It became my routine an evening walk along the shore.

People came and went, joggers, lovers, families each lost in their own rhythm.
And I'd Walk among them, barefoot on the wet sand, watching the sunset melt into the waves.

I didn't wait for anyone now. But sometimes, when the sea breeze brushed against my hair, I'd feel like he was walking beside me again.

Invisible, but present.

The gulls cried above, and I whispered softly, "We're still walking, Aditya. Just in different worlds."

One day, months after the award, I visited a local bookstore. On a quiet corner shelf, there was a small stack of *Let's Walk.*

A young man and woman stood nearby, flipping through copies.

The girl said, "This story feels so real. It's like someone lived it."

The boy smiled. "Maybe they did."

I wanted to tell them *we did*. But I just smiled, picked up a copy, and left it signed anonymously on the table:

*"Keep walking. – M."*

As I walked out, I heard the girl gasp softly, "Look, it's signed!"

And that made me smile wider.

Because somewhere, somehow, our story had found new walkers.

It took me four years to return to Bangalore.

I went back to Bangalore. Everything looked the same and different at once. The skyline taller, the roads wider, but the rhythm… that quiet hum of Bangalore life still there, soft and stubborn.

I took a cab to Ulsoor lake Koramangala, tracing the same routes we had once walked. The driver was humming a Kannada song, the same one I used to hear from Aditya's headphones. It almost felt like the city was playing our memories back to me one line, one turn, one heartbeat at a time. When the cab turned onto the old street, I asked him to stop. I got out and stood still.

There it was the Gul mohar tree.

Time had thickened its branches, and its flowers had spilled like embers across the sidewalk. The sight alone made my throat tighten.

Across the road, the old building still stood his apartment, the balcony where he'd once stood with coffee, watching the world wake. The windows were closed now, curtains drawn, a quiet stillness behind them.

I crossed the road slowly, each step heavier than the last.

A new tenant lived there now, a young couple. They had plants by the window too little green lives stretching toward sunlight, like hope reinvented.

I didn't knock. I didn't need to.

This wasn't a visit of presence; it was a visit of memory.

I sat on the low compound wall under the Gul mohar. From my bag, I took out two things his old notebook, and the infinity ring Aditi had returned to me.

The notebook was filled with my handwriting now parts of *Let's Walk*, drafts, stray thoughts. It had lived two lives his and mine.

I opened it to the last page, the one I had left blank after finishing the book.

I uncapped my pen and wrote slowly, carefully:

*"We did walk, Aditya. Maybe not together in the world's eyes, but every word, every breath I take carries you still. The path didn't end it just bent into forever."*

I smiled, placed the ring on top of that page, and closed the book. The infinity loop glimmered faintly in the dappled sunlight, like it understood what I was doing.

It began to drizzle. Of course it did. It always rained when something ended, or maybe when something began. I slipped off my sandals and walked barefoot down the lane. The wet ground felt cool, grounding.

Every corner held a piece of us. The small café where he once ordered coffee "extra strong, less sugar." The narrow alley where we once took shelter from rain. The park bench where we sat and spoke about nothing and everything.

I didn't cry.

Grief, after all, had changed shape. It had turned into gratitude.

I whispered quietly, "We're still walking, aren't we?"

The wind answered, carrying the smell of rain-soaked flowers.

As I turned the corner, I saw a man and woman young, laughing, standing under the same Gul mohar tree. The boy was holding out an umbrella, his eyes shy.

And then, in that soft drizzle, he said those two familiar words: "Let's Walk?"

The girl smiled and nodded, slipping her hand into his.

I froze for a moment. It was the same tone, the same cadence. I almost laughed through the tears that rose in my eyes. The city, it seemed, had a way of recycling magic old words to new lovers, old dreams to new beginnings. I watched them walk away, their silhouettes dissolving into the misty rain. And for the first time, I felt peace.

That evening, I took a late flight back to Mumbai. The clouds below looked like sheets of cotton, endless and white. I watched the horizon that eternal line between sky and earth, day and night, then and now.

Maybe Aditya was right. Maybe love isn't about staying together; maybe it's about continuing the walk, even when the other person isn't beside you.

Because as long as you're still walking remembering, growing, writing the love is still alive somewhere in the universe.

When the plane touched down, I didn't rush out. I sat there for a minute longer, eyes closed, whispering,

"Thank you for walking with me, Aditya."

***

A few months later, I released a special edition of *Let's Walk.* It had an author's note the only time I wrote directly, as Mira.

*"This story was never about endings. It was about continuity. About two people who kept walking even when time separated them. About love that learned to exist in silence."*

*"For Aditya, who taught me that sometimes, the most beautiful journeys never really end."*

The first copy was placed in a bookstore in Bangalore, near MG Road, where it had all begun. I left a small note inside that copy, folded between the pages:

*"If you ever find this, keep walking. – Mira."*

That night, I walked along Marine Drive the sea shimmering under streetlights, the city breathing behind me. I carried no phone, no bag, no plans just the calm weight of memory. A soft breeze played with my hair. Somewhere, music from a roadside café drifted a song in Kannada, one he used to hum absentmindedly. I smiled, tears glistening but gentle. Somewhere beyond this world, I hoped he was smiling too. Maybe he'd found his peace. Maybe he was still walking, waiting for me.

As I sat on the sea wall, I whispered the line that had once started it all: "Let's Walk?"

But this time, it wasn't a question. It was a promise to life, to love, to memory. A promise to keep walking through pages, through time, through everything that connects one soul to another. The sea roared quietly, the sky dimmed to silver, and for a moment, I felt him beside me again not as a ghost, but as a gentle rhythm within my heart.

Years later, when readers ask me why *Let's Walk* feels so real, I smile.

Some say it's because I understand emotions deeply.

Some say it's because I've experienced loss.

Some even say it's because I'm a romantic at heart.

But the truth — the real twist — is simple:

It *was* real.

It *is* real.

There was a man named Aditya.

There was a girl named Mira.

They met, they walked, they parted.

And then one of them wrote their story, from the other's eyes.

Because when love can no longer live in reality, it survives in words.

So, if you ever find yourself walking alone some evening, and you hear the faint whisper of two words carried by the breeze *Let's walk?* know that it's not just an echo.

It's us.

Still walking.

# EPILOGUE

It's been five years since the launch of *Let's Walk.* Five years since I stood under that soft yellow light, reading aloud a story that wasn't just mine.

The world moved on, as it always does. The book lived its own quiet life translated, quoted, underlined in yellow highlighters by strangers who saw themselves in our words.

I never wrote another novel. Not because I had nothing left to say but because *that* story had said everything. I started teaching creative writing instead. Every time my students asked, "How do you write something that feels real?" I told them, "You don't write it. You live it first."

And then, one quiet Sunday morning, something unexpected happened.

My email inbox was cluttered with the usual thing's student drafts, newsletters, event invites.

But one message stood out. The subject line simply read: "Found something that belongs to you."

Curious, I clicked.

*"Dear Myra Sharma (or should I say, Mira),*

*I don't know if this will reach you, but I hope it does. I'm writing from Bangalore. I found a copy of your book 'Let's Walk' in a small bookstore near MG Road. There was a note inside, folded between pages 187 and 188. It said 'If you ever find this, keep walking. – Mira.'*

*I wanted you to know that your words found me at the right time. I had just lost someone I loved, and reading this story felt like walking beside a memory instead of running from it.*

*So, thank you, not just for the book, but for the feeling that maybe we never really lose the people who walk with us for a while.*

*Warmly,*
*Arjun."*

I read it twice. Then a third time.

Something inside me shifted that old familiar warmth, the kind that feels like someone whispering across time: *You, see? The story still walks.*

I sat at my desk for a long while before replying.

*"Dear Arjun,*

*Thank you for your message. You didn't find something that belongs to me, you found something that belongs to all of us. The note was left for anyone who needed to remember that love isn't about arrival or departure. It's about the walk in between.*

*I'm glad it found you when you needed it. That's all I ever wanted the story to do — to walk a little further, with someone else.*

*Keep walking.*

*– Mira."*

When I hit send, I realized I was smiling through quiet tears. Not the heavy kind that ache, but the gentle kind that remind your life has meaning after all.

Two months later, I visited Bangalore again for a literary panel. The organizers had arranged a talk at the very same bookstore on MG Road the one where Arjun had found my note. When I walked in, the bell above the door jingled the same soft metallic sound from years ago. The shelves were neatly lined, the air smelled faintly of paper and rain.

A young man approached me after the session, holding a worn-out copy of *Let's Walk.*

He smiled. "You must be Mira."

It was Arjun.

He looked familiar in the way kind people do calm eyes, gentle presence.

"This book…" he said quietly, "…it saved me."

I didn't know what to say. Words, for once, felt unnecessary.

He opened to the page where my old note was still tucked in, its edges frayed. "I kept it safe. I thought you might want it back."

I looked at him, then shook my head. "No. You keep it. That note found you for a reason."

He nodded slowly, understanding without questions. "Then maybe I'll pass it forward one day."

And just like that, I knew the circle had widened again.

After the event, I took the metro back, MG Road to Baiyappanahalli. The same route. The same stations.

The city had changed, yes, but the rhythm remained: the faint metallic hum, the mixed chatter, the soft announcements in four languages.

I found myself smiling at small details, a man asleep against the window, a child giggling at his reflection, a woman humming to herself.

And for a moment, I saw him there, Aditya, leaning against the door, half-smile on his face, eyes lost in thought.

The doors closed, the train moved, and I whispered under my breath, "Still walking."

Before leaving the city, I stopped by the Gul mohar tree one last time.

The branches were heavier now, roots sprawling deeper into the ground. Beneath it, the earth was still marked with fallen red petals bright, defiant, alive.

From my bag, I took out something small, a new notebook. On its first page, I wrote:

*"Every story is a continuation. If you found this, maybe you were meant to."*

And on the second page, in the same handwriting that had once changed my life, I wrote just two words:

*"Let's walk?"*

I left it there, on the bench under the tree, where someone new might one day find it.

That evening, as the flight lifted from Bangalore, I looked down through the small oval window.

People often say love ends. But I've learned something different.

Love doesn't end; it transfers. It moves from one heart to another, from one story to another, from one lifetime to the next.

And if you're lucky, it leaves behind a note that says, *keep walking.*

When I reached home that night, I placed my old copy of *Let's Walk* on the shelf beside a framed photograph of the sea. The window was open. The city outside was quiet, the waves steady and rhythmic.

And just as I turned off the lights, I heard it, not a sound, but a feeling, like air shifting softly through time.

A whisper, gentle and familiar.

*"Let's walk?"*

I smiled in the dark. "Always."

Years from now, someone will pick up this book, not knowing who Aditya or Mira were. They'll read it as fiction a story of two strangers who met in a city and changed each other's lives.

And that's fine. Because what matters isn't whether they believe it's real.

What matters is that, for a while, it made them feel something real.

Maybe they'll think of someone they once walked with.

Maybe they'll send a message.

Maybe they'll just step outside, look up at the sky, and whisper the words that began it all.

And somewhere, wherever stories go when they're done, we'll hear it again.

That soft, unending invitation.

*Let's walk.*

## A Message from Prakash Kannan

Thank you for walking alongside Aditya on this journey. I hope you found a piece of your own rhythm here.

It has been an honor to share Aditya's story with you. I sincerely hope to see you for the next one.

Find me online at www.prakashkannan.com

Write your feedback to e-mail: 7prakashkannan@gmail.com

www.ingramcontent.com/pod-product-compliance
Lightning Source LLC
Chambersburg PA
CBHW062104160726
48282CB00026B/670
* 9 7 8 9 3 5 4 6 9 0 4 2 6 *